FOLLOW the MONEY

PETER CORRIS is known as the 'godfather' of Australian crime fiction through his Cliff Hardy detective stories. He has written in many other areas, including a co-authored autobiography of the late Professor Fred Hollows, a history of boxing in Australia, spy novels, historical novels and a collection of short stories about golf (see petercorris.net). In 2009, Peter Corris was awarded the Ned Kelly Award for Best Fiction by the Crime Writers Association of Australia. He is married to writer Jean Bedford and has lived in Sydney for most of his life. They have three daughters.

PETER CORRIS

FOLLOW the MONEY

ALLEN&UNWIN

Thanks to Helen Barnes, Jean Bedford, Ruth Corris,
Jo Jarrah and Stephen Wallace.

First published by Allen & Unwin in 2011
Copyright © Peter Corris 2011

Allen & Unwin
83 Alexander Street
Crows Nest NSW 2065
Australia
Phone: (61 2) 8425 0100
Fax: (61 2) 9906 2218
Email: info@allenandunwin.com
Web: www.allenandunwin.com

Cataloguing-in-Publication details are available
from the National Library of Australia
www.trove.nla.gov.au

ISBN 978 1 74237 379 9

Internal text design by Emily O'Neill
Set in 12/17 pt Adobe Caslon by Midland Typesetters, Australia
Printed and bound in Australia by Griffin Press

10 9 8 7 6 5 4 3 2 1

MIX
Paper from
responsible sources
FSC® C009448
www.fsc.org

The paper in this book is FSC certified.
FSC promotes environmentally responsible,
socially beneficial and economically viable
management of the world's forests.

For Gaby Naher

For money has a power above
The stars and fate to manage love

Samuel Butler

part one

1

'I heard about your misfortune,' Miles Standish said. 'That's why I asked to see you.'

'I've had a few misfortunes in my time,' I said. 'Which one d'you mean?'

'Losing all your money.'

'Oh, that one.'

Standish was a lawyer. His secretary had rung me at home that morning asking me to meet him at his office at two in the afternoon. When I asked what about she said Mr Standish would explain. He'd told her to tell me that the matter was important, urgent and the meeting would be of mutual benefit.

I had nothing better to do and since I didn't have a private investigator's licence anymore and the money I'd inherited from Lily Truscott—and there was a lot left of it even after some house fixing and gifts and loans here and there—had all gone, 'mutual benefit' had an appealing ring.

Standish's office was in Edgecliff and I travelled there from Glebe by bus, two buses. Driving in Sydney had become an exercise in frustration. Since my heart attack and bypass, I'd been advised to avoid stress and I found off-peak bus travel restful. I was early and I sat in the park on a cool late autumn day looking around at things that had changed and were going to change more. The boxing stadium where Freddie Dawson had cast a pall over Sydney's sporting community by knocking out Vic Patrick had long gone, and the White City tennis courts were no longer grass. Boats bobbed on the water as they had since 1788 and always would, but if the climate change gurus were right, where I was sitting would be underwater later this century. How much later?

Standish's office was one level up in a building on New South Head Road. The façade was nineteenth century but the interior was twentieth, even twenty-first—carpet, pastel walls, air-conditioning, pot plants. The secretary who'd summoned me was there to greet me. Obviously head honcho of a group of three women, all busy in the open-plan office, she was Asian, elegant and with a private school accent.

'Thank you for being so prompt, Mr Hardy. Mr Standish is anxious to see you.'

Anxious didn't seem quite the right word for these surroundings. Back when I had a low-rent office in Newtown, anxious was just the right word—my clients were anxious and so was I. Here, comfortable seemed more the go, but comfort is easily disturbed.

She showed me into a room that almost made the outer office look shabby. It was all teak and glass and set up for both work and relaxation—a huge desk holding electronic equipment reminiscent of NASA, and a cosy arrangement of armchairs, discreet wet bar and coffee table tucked away in a corner. The waist- to almost ceiling-high windows looked out onto the main road but the double-glazing muted the traffic noise to an agreeable hum.

Standish sprang from behind the desk, rounded it athletically, and almost bounded towards me. He was tall, well built, and looked about thirty, which could have meant he was older trying to look younger or younger trying to look older. He wore the regulation blue shirt and burgundy tie, dark trousers. We shook hands—firm grip, a golfer maybe.

'Have a seat. Coffee?'

'No. Thanks. Nice place. Did someone refer you to me?'

'Not exactly.'

Standish liked to talk, especially about himself. He told me he wasn't a courtroom lawyer. He hadn't been in one since moot court in his student days. He was a money lawyer. I already knew that. You don't turn up for a meeting like this without doing some checking.

'I put together people,' he said. 'And then I put together deals. I help the money to be found and placed where it's needed to the benefit of all parties including myself. You must know the movie *Chinatown*.'

'I do.'

'One of our . . . one of my favourites. You'll remember Jake Gittes says divorce work is his metier. Deals are mine. I got first class honours in contract law and graduated magna cum laude from the Yale MBA course. I know the Cayman Islands, Cook Islands, Isle of Man, Jersey and Australian tax acts off by heart.'

I said, 'Can't leave you much room to know anything else.'

He leaned back. 'You'd be surprised. I know you failed contract law at the University of New South Wales and abandoned your studies. I know that you are banned for life from holding a private enquiry agent's licence in New South Wales and, by extension, anywhere in Australia. I know you had investments worth several hundred thousand dollars and it has all gone.'

I shrugged. 'I never felt good about being rich anyway.'

'How do you feel about being bankrupt?'

'It's not that bad.'

'It will be, and soon.'

He brought a computer to life and tapped the keys. 'Let me see if I've got this right. Richard Malouf was a partner in the very honest and upright firm that controlled your financial affairs. Unhappily, he was neither honest nor upright. Because of your, shall I say, careless attitude to your assets, he was able, over time, to liquidate the majority of your shares and hive off the money to accounts he controlled.'

I sighed. 'I don't really want to hear this. Malouf gambled the money away and got himself shot when he ran up a tab with someone who got impatient first and then got angry. You're right; when I inherited some money I took my business to an accounting firm someone had recommended: a big firm.'

Standish smiled. 'A mistake as it turned out. You should've come to me.'

Not likely, I thought, but he was accurate. I met the boss of the accounting firm—a Lebanese Australian named Perry Hassan—and liked him. He introduced me to Malouf. We talked; he seemed to understand my diffidence about being a capitalist investor. I trusted him. Financial matters bore me. I signed things I shouldn't have and put things away in a drawer unopened.

'Spilt milk,' I said. 'The money's gone.'

'What if I told you it isn't, not necessarily.'

'There was a thorough investigation.'

'How many thorough investigations have you known that were all complete bullshit?'

He had my interest now, not because I believed him, but because the smooth unflappability was fraying. Despite the air-conditioning, he looked a little damp around the edges.

'You've got a point, but Malouf's dead. He was identified by his wife.'

'Dental records? DNA? Did they bring in the Bali ID unit?'

'I don't know.'

'They didn't. There was a big stink on about a murdered family and they were preoccupied. He's not dead. He's been spotted.'

'So has Lord Lucan. So has Elvis.'

'This is reliable information. I want to hire you to catch him.'

'Why would I do that? The money's gone.'

'I don't believe it. I think the gambling was a cover story to help convince the authorities that he was dead. He's still got your money, or some of it. Plus that of a lot of other people who could be very grateful to you.'

I looked around the room—the framed certificates, the photographs in the company of celebrities in politics, sport and show business, the gleaming surfaces. Standish was the living embodiment of a business and lifestyle I disliked. He was right about me failing contract law. I'd detested the subject and wrote rude things about the questions and teachers before walking out. It had been a catalyst for my giving up university and doing other things. I didn't want to work for this man.

Standish tapped some more keys. 'Following on from what I said about your finances, it'll interest you to learn that Malouf left you a little legacy. More of a time bomb really. He bought, in your name, a parcel of shares at what seemed bargain rates. You OK'd the purchase. It was peanuts as things stood in your portfolio then. However, those are what's called option shares and holders are liable for a very substantial margin call on them. In about a month's time you're looking at a bill for three hundred thousand dollars, give or take.'

I felt a sharp prick of anxiety. Being short of money was one thing, and something I knew a bit about. But bankruptcy was something else. And if what Standish said was true, Malouf hadn't just taken me for a ride like the others but had got personal. When someone gets personal with me I get personal back.

He gave me a Hollywood smile. 'I thought that'd get your attention. To answer your question, there's your motivation. Catch Malouf and some very serious charges can be brought against him. You might be able to make a case of fraudulent dealing on his part that could get you off the hook in respect of the shares. I could help you with that, really help. Worst case scenario—if you can recover the money from Malouf, you could pay the call. The shares will have value in time, although not quite yet, given the GFC.'

'And would you help me with that?'

'What?'

'Recovering the money from Malouf.'

The smile again, broader. 'I wouldn't stand in your way.'

'How do I know you're not lying about the shares?'

9

He opened a drawer in the desk and slid a sheet of paper across to me. 'I got in touch with Perry Hassan, your trusted friend. He confirmed what I've just told you.'

I read Perry's email to Standish. Somehow Malouf's purchase of the shares, on the positive side of the ledger, hadn't cost enough initially to make a difference to my balance sheet, but Perry conceded that I was facing bankruptcy. We civilians imagine that information about clients held by financial advisers is private and protected, but these days nothing is. At a guess, Standish had some leverage on Perry.

'I have a few questions,' I said.

'Of course.'

'I don't have an investigator's licence.'

'From what I've heard of your conduct as a PEA, the rules you broke and the lines you stepped over, that hardly matters.'

'That's a fair point. OK, the real question. You've got a million-dollar office and a secretary who's probably as efficient as she is glamorous. You know Mel Gibson and Bob Carr and Greg Norman; but you strike me as just a bit worried. What's *your* motivation, Mr Standish?'

2

Suddenly Standish looked closer to forty than thirty. His face seemed to clench and lines radiated out from his eyes.

'Did you ever meet Malouf?' he said.

'Two or three times.'

'What did you think of him?'

I didn't want to talk about Malouf. I'd tried to forget him. 'As I said, I found all that money management stuff boring and I tended not to take much notice of the people who spouted it.'

He persisted. 'Good-looking?'

'Certainly not ugly, anyway.'

'He had . . . has a fatal attraction for women, including my wife.'

You want to say 'Ah' at times like that but you don't.

'I discovered that they'd been having a long-running affair.'

'How did you discover that?'

'She told me.'

It hurt him to say it; Standish was the sort of man who liked to put a personal-positive spin on anything. 'Why?'

'It was after he disappeared with your money and other people's as well, as I suppose you know. She seemed upset at the news about Malouf but not distraught. But it was a sort of catalyst. We hadn't been getting along for some time, the usual things . . . and she told me, shouted it to me. She said she loved him.'

Saying this had taken a lot out of him. He got up and the athletic bounce had left him as he crossed to where his bar fridge and a cupboard were tucked away. 'I'm going to have a drink. You?'

It was about three hours before my usual drinking time, but I didn't want him to feel any worse than he already did. 'Sure, what've you got?'

'Everything.'

'Scotch, a bit of ice.'

I didn't recognise the bottle; that doesn't mean much; I don't see enough single malts to get well acquainted. He made the drinks and brought the bottle back to the desk. The whisky was smooth—about as far as my capacity for appreciation goes. Standish downed half of his in a swallow and topped up his glass.

'I'm not a drunk,' he said.

'No.'

'Just that it's hard to . . . relive it all.'

'Yes.'

'Are you making fun of me?'

I sipped the drink. 'No, I'm not. But you've only scratched the surface of what you want to tell me about all this, and I'm wondering how much you're going to have to drink to get through it.'

He pushed the glass away. 'They told me you were a hard man to deal with, but that if I was straight with you you'd give me a hearing and might be willing to help.'

'I wouldn't exactly call what you've been doing up to now being straight.'

'No, you're right. I'm sorry. I'm manipulative—force of habit. Let's start again.'

Standish said his wife, Felicity, had met Malouf at a dinner for people in what he called the finance industry where he was the keynote speaker.

'I was swamped by commitments, clients, prospective clients, offers of various kinds.' He pointed to his glass. 'I'd had a few too many.'

'It happens,' I said.

'Yeah. I tell myself if not that night, then sometime, and if not him, someone else. I sort of believe it. Anyway, the point is, it became an affair. I was busy and didn't know until she hit me with it.'

'You said she was only upset when Malouf was killed, not devastated.'

'You'll think me paranoid, but I suspect her and Malouf's wife and Christ knows who else of being involved in a conspiracy. There's a lot of money involved, but more than that . . .'

For a man like Standish that was a big admission. What could be 'more' than money? I sipped whisky and waited for him to tell me.

'Word got around about Felicity's involvement with Malouf. Confidence is everything in this business. Trust is nothing. A few clients have . . . withdrawn; a few are cooling off and it's not just the GFC. I'm facing a *personal* fucking financial crisis.'

So it was about reputation but still about money. He was serious, no question. He'd drawn up a list of names—the person who claimed to have seen Malouf, Malouf's wife, his own wife, gamblers the police had interviewed, a journalist who'd covered the case, a lawyer representing a client who was suing Perry Hassan's firm and another who was processing Perry's application to the insurance company covering him against precisely this kind of disaster. For someone who didn't particularly care for lawyers, it looked as though I was going to be spending some time with them. *If* I agreed to work for Standish.

'Well?' he said after handing over the list and some supporting information—newspaper clippings, web page printouts, emails. 'Will you help me, and yourself?'

I finished the drink and ran my eye over the list. The

alleged sighting had been in Middle Harbour, at a marina by the Spit Bridge. That helped me to decide. It'd be hard enough tracking people down and questioning them with no credentials whatsoever in Sydney, but impossible in Liechtenstein or the Bahamas. Standish saw me focusing on that entry.

'He's still in Sydney. That means there's a reason, probably an associate. He had to have someone help him mount this operation.'

'From what you've said it could be a woman looking after him, giving him sanctuary. That's if the sighting's genuine.'

'The names are there. Felicity and I are separated. You can approach her.'

'The helpful associate and the woman could be one and the same,' I said.

'Does that mean you're in?'

'I'm thinking about it.'

'Let's talk money.'

Standish began by mentioning a contract, a daily rate and expenses but I stopped him.

'First off, I'll go and see this yachtsman, the one who says he saw Malouf. If he doesn't convince me then it's all off and I won't charge you anything. If I'm convinced I'll follow up the other leads and see where I get. I'll charge you what I think the work's worth.'

'That's not businesslike.'

'Right,' I said, 'look where businesslike has got us. I'll need your email address and a mobile number where I can reach you twenty-four seven.'

He slumped down in his chair. 'See May Ling in the office.'

I dealt with May Ling, who seemed to have everything at her perfectly manicured fingertips. I went down the stairs to the street feeling strangely buoyant. It wasn't just the prospect of recovering some money or avoiding bankruptcy. High enough stakes to start with, but it was more than that. It was because I was working again and about to be useful in a way I hadn't been for too long. Maybe.

They told me that after the heart operation I'd have a new surge of energy, feel ten years younger. I did some days, not others. Some days I worried about little things that never used to bother me and some days I didn't let quite big things concern me at all. And I couldn't predict the way it'd go. For the moment I *was* feeling younger because of the prospect of interesting work. I decided to walk back to the city for the exercise and to plan ahead. I was looking forward to studying the material Standish had given me and interviewing Stefan Nordlung, who'd claimed to have seen Malouf. He was a retired marine engineer, an acquaintance of Malouf's. A drive to Seaforth tomorrow morning was a pleasant prospect after all the sitting about and time-filling I'd been doing.

I'd covered several kilometres briskly and was feeling good when my mobile buzzed. For some reason I have an aversion to walking along with the thing cocked up at my ear the way so many people do. I stopped and stepped out of the way to take the call.

'Cliff, it's Megan.'

My daughter. 'Yes, love?'

'Good news.'

'Always welcome. Tell me.'

'I'm pregnant.'

I said 'What?' so loudly people in the street gave me an alarmed look.

'I said I'm going to have a baby.'

'I can't believe it.'

'Why? Didn't you think Hank and I were fucking?'

That was pure Megan—direct. 'Yes, but . . . Well, that's terrific. When?'

'Six months. We waited until we were completely sure. We phoned Hank's people in the States and you're the first to know here.'

I mumbled something, said I'd see her that night and walked on in a sort of daze. Fatherhood had been sprung on me; I hadn't known of Megan's existence until she was eighteen. Now this. I didn't know what a grandfather's credentials were, but I was pretty sure they didn't include bankruptcy. I thought about it as I moved on. Megan was young, who knew how many kids she might have and what help she might need? The stakes just climbed higher.

3

The happy couple were so involved in what they were doing—and they behaved as though they'd achieved something no one else in the world had ever done—that they didn't ask me what I was up to. That suited me. Like them, I wanted to be sure before making any announcements. I was happy for them and myself: I'd missed out on the real experience of fatherhood, a big thing to miss out on, and now I was getting a second chance at a version of it.

I went home from their flat with two-thirds of a bottle of champagne inside me. Megan wasn't drinking and Hank was almost too excited to drink. The walk from Newtown to Glebe sobered me and it wasn't late. Time to work.

I transferred Standish's list and his brief comments on the people on it into a notebook. I had names—Stefan Nordlung, Felicity Standish, Rosemary Malouf, Prospero Sabatini, Clive Finn and Selim Houli. Sabatini was the journalist who'd written on the Malouf matter; Finn and Houli were gamblers. Finn was the manager of a casino at Parramatta and Houli ran a nightclub and a high stakes card game at Kings Cross. Both men had told police that Malouf had lost heavily but both denied having anything to do with his disappearance. I had addresses and phone numbers for some of them. I spread the clippings, printouts and emails on the desk in the room I used as an office—now given over mainly to paying bills—and immersed myself in the life and times of Richard Malouf.

Perry Hassan had sent Standish a copy of the CV Malouf had provided when applying successfully for a job in his firm. This, with Sabatini's published articles, provided a detailed portrait. Richard Malouf was thirty-five, the only son of immigrant Lebanese parents who'd come to Australia in the early 1970s. Malouf senior was a veterinarian not qualified to practise in Australia but who acquired a great reputation among the Brisbane horse racing fraternity. He did well and his son attended private schools. Both parents were now dead. Richard Malouf played soccer for the school and was scouted by professional clubs. Instead, after stellar HSC results, he went to the University of Western Australia where he got a degree in economics. He followed with a master's in computer science and worked for IBM and other firms in Perth before coming east and joining Perry Hassan's outfit.

In 2003 he married Rosemary Bruce, an airline flight attendant. They had no children, lived in Balmain with a water view and a mortgage, and shared a Beemer. Malouf played golf at Kogarah, amateur soccer briefly, and collected wine. He was found in his car at the Sydney airport parking station. He'd been shot once through the head.

Several photographs accompanied Sabatini's articles—schoolboy Malouf with his near perfect HSC score, Malouf with the soccer ball on a string and later receiving an award at IBM. I worked through the material, highlighting various points and making notes. I put the stuff together neatly and got up to take the medications I'd be taking for the rest of my life for blood pressure, heart rhythm regulation, cholesterol control. I swallowed them down with the dregs of the red wine I'd been drinking as an aid to concentration. It was a life sentence, but not to do it was a death sentence.

Always get up from your studies with a question, someone had said. I had one: why would a high flyer like Malouf join a firm like Perry Hassan's? It was big, but not the biggest.

In the morning I phoned Nordlung at his home address. A woman with a faint American accent answered and I told her what I wanted.

'I'm his wife. You'll find him at the marina by the Spit Bridge, working on his boat.'

'Can you tell me the name of the boat, Mrs Nordlung?'

'It's the *Gretchen III*—that's Stefan's little joke. Gretchen's my name and I'm his third wife.'

I couldn't be sure but she sounded drunk. At that time in the morning? Well, it happens.

It was a perfect day with a blue sky and light wind. Coming down Spit Road towards the water gave me a multi-million dollar view of Middle Harbour—no house with that view would be worth under a million and the boats would add many, many noughts. It was Wednesday mid-morning and the traffic was light, but there was plenty of activity around the launching ramps and at the marina and not much parking space. I squeezed in between two massive SUVs and remembered to watch my shins on their towing attachments. Tough for some—if you couldn't afford a marina berth you had to keep your boat in the garage and tow it here.

The marina was T-shaped and the boats varied from modest little numbers to monsters with lofty flagpoles and garden boxes on the decks. I paused to take in the scene and when I thought of the insurance premiums and the upkeep and all the fees involved, it suddenly seemed that I wasn't looking at boats but at huge, floating bundles of money. I asked at the office where the *Gretchen III* was and the woman pointed and then looked closely at me.

'Are you from the police?'

'No, why?'

'I just thought . . .'

Looking in the direction she'd indicated, about halfway down the jetty, I could see people gathered around, staring down at a moored boat. I heard sirens wailing and I hurried. Attracting all the attention was a sleek boat with *Gretchen III* painted in blue on its white hull. Two men were bending over a man lying on the deck. One of the men had a mobile phone to his ear. The man on the deck was still; water was dribbling from his clothes and his head was cocked at an odd angle. There was a tangle of rope around his left leg.

The crowd was murmuring and one man swore as he saw another taking pictures with his mobile phone.

'What happened?' I asked the picture snapper as he backed away.

'Looks like he got caught up somehow, fell in and drowned. I've gotta get this off to the media.'

The sirens screamed, people jumped aside, and an ambulance and a police vehicle drove down the jetty. There was an eerie silence as the sirens died, broken only by the slapping of the water against the boats and the pylons and the flapping of the flags on the masts. The paramedics jumped down onto the deck and the men who'd been attending the victim moved aside. I got a good look at him —long-limbed, long-headed with pale blonde hair matted against his skull. His pale eyes stared sightlessly at the sky.

I hung around picking up snippets of information. Nordlung had been found by the owner of the boat berthed alongside his, about twenty minutes before I got there.

He'd noticed how untidy the deck of the *Gretchen III* was and had gone aboard to investigate. Nordlung was famous for keeping his boat in pristine condition. He found the rope running from where it had caught on the hatch door over the side. When he hauled on it, the body came into view. Nordlung was a big man and it had taken two to get him on the deck. They tried to resuscitate him but failed.

The police spoke to the two yachtsmen who were both smoking and looking shaken. Then there was a flurry of activity as the police used their mobile phones and pushed the onlookers further away. Another car arrived with plainclothes detectives and the chequered tape came out indicating that this was a crime scene. The detectives began taking names and addresses and I drifted away to the edge of the growing crowd. Eventually, I was able to walk away with others whose interest had been satisfied.

I bought a coffee at a stall outside the marina and drank it leaning against my car in the sunshine. More official vehicles arrived—SOC people, water police with, at a guess, a frogman, and there was probably a pathologist in the mix. A television camera crew swept in.

Shit happens, as they say, and there was no necessary connection between Nordlung's death and my visit. For all I knew he could've had a hundred enemies, but it seemed more than likely there was a connection. The question then was, who knew of my intention? Standish, but not the precise time. Nordlung's wife. The other possibility was that Nordlung's phone was tapped and that can never be ruled out with the surveillance equipment around now. That idea opened up other questions. If Malouf had faked his death, someone had died to provide the body. And now Nordlung. They must be playing for higher stakes here than just ripping off some middle-range investors.

Thinking hard, I drove back to the city to a car park near the building where Prospero Sabatini worked. He wrote for a weekly called *The Investor*, which prided itself on its investigative journalism. I'd Googled him and got the essential details—aged thirty-two, ex-army with service in Timor and the Solomon Islands, master's degree in economics, keen rock climber. He'd published two books—one on corporate fraud, one on rock climbing. I phoned Sabatini and he agreed to meet me for lunch in a pub close by.

I called Standish's mobile and was told that it was either switched off or out of range. He was living in a serviced apartment in Potts Point. I called the direct line to his flat and got the standard Telstra voice message. I asked him to call me as soon as possible. Then I phoned Standish's office and got May Ling.

'It's Cliff Hardy. Mr Standish, please.'

'I'm afraid Mr Standish isn't available, Mr Hardy.'

She made it sound as if she was doing me a favour giving me this information.

'Why?'

'He's away on business.'

'Where? For how long?'

'I'm not at liberty to say.'

'It's important. How can I reach him?'

'I can't help you. I'm sorry. I'll tell him you called.'

'When?'

'When he returns.'

'I hope you can keep everything running smoothly until then.'

'I think so. Goodbye.'

I just bet you can, I thought.

A frustrating morning, requiring a relaxation of a rule. I went to the pub Sabatini had nominated, the John Curtin, and ordered a middy of Pure Blonde—low carb, nothing you couldn't work off in a gym session. Sabatini's photograph, postage stamp-size, had appeared at the top of his articles and I had no trouble recognising him when he strolled into the pub. The surprise was that he seemed to recognise me. We shook hands.

'We've met, sort of,' he said.

He was short-medium, neatly put together, with dark hair and a beard. He wore the clothes favoured by some in his profession—suit, dark shirt, dark tie loosely knotted. I couldn't place him.

'I worked with Lily Truscott on a few things a while back. I was at the wake.'

I nodded. 'It's a bit of a blur to me now. What're you drinking?'

He ordered red wine and I had one as well to go with the pasta. We ate at an outside table in Liverpool Street. I told Sabatini more or less the truth—that I'd been hired by someone who believed that Richard Malouf was still alive and wanted redress. No name, of course. I said that the person who'd claimed to have seen Malouf after his reported death was also dead. I said I'd read his articles and thought he'd be interested if any of this turned out to be true.

'You bet I'd be interested.'

'Did you have any reason to think the death might've been faked?'

'No, he was a notorious gambler and womaniser. Any number of people could've been out to get him.'

'But an execution seems a bit . . . extreme.'

'I did think that at the time, and I did wonder why he hadn't taken the Qantas option when he'd got hold of the money. You can gamble and fuck in comfort just about anywhere.'

'If you were at the wake you must know about me. They took away my PEA licence. I've got no standing. Malouf stripped me of a fair bit of money, but here's something in your line—he left me with a bunch of shares that have a big call on them. I'm facing bankruptcy. That's my interest, plus it was Lily's money, really. I was trying to do a bit of good with it here and there. I'm angry.'

That was coming it a bit strong, but I needed his help and I can be manipulative when I have to be. We both worked on the pasta and the wine for a few minutes while the foot traffic drifted past us.

I said, 'If this thing takes shape you'll get whatever I have to give.'

He scooped up the last of his ravioli and took a sip of the wine. 'Thanks. I can understand where you're coming from. But how can I help now?'

'We've got two dead people connected to this—possibly. I've got the feeling that there's much more to the Malouf thing than meets the eye.'

He drained his glass. 'You're right there, Cliff. Much more.'

4

Sabatini stretched, easing a back that spent too long rigid in front of a computer screen. 'What happened at Hassan and Associates isn't an isolated incident. The Malouf case has . . . tentacles. I get whispers that quite a lot of small and medium range businesses are in trouble. There's been a lot of borrowing and shoring up, which is expensive in the current climate. There's also been a fair bit of apparent cyber fraud. Disappearing money. Mostly, it's kept quiet and insurance covers the losses. The firms compensate over and above the lost amount on the proviso that the details don't get out. The servers and the credit company people don't want publicity. The Malouf case made an exception because it was too big to be dealt with in house, as it were, and he turned up dead, but believe me, there's a collection of Malouf types floating about playing games with other people's money.'

'The insurance companies must be getting shitty.'

'Yes, and no. In most cases, in real terms the amounts aren't that big, and the legal insurers lay off against insurers and spread the pain down the line and pretty thin. They know they're being taken advantage of but what can they do? They want to keep the lid on it and stay in business. No one who's ever been broken into, had a car damaged or lost anything has any sympathy for insurance companies. They use the excess clause to cover their arses and they make millions by investing the policy premiums, most of which they never have to pay out on. Insurance is a legal racket.'

'I wouldn't argue with you, but . . .'

'When you contacted me just now I thought you might have been hired by one of the insurers to investigate, break the code of silence, but unless you're bullshitting me this is all new to you.'

'It is. I started in at a very small scale. I thought it was just a rip-off missing person scam with a twist—the missing party apparently dead. But it seems to be growing hour by hour. How do you know as much as you do?'

'Sealed containers leak.'

'Do you have names for these other embezzlers?'

A waiter cleared our table and asked if we wanted anything else.

'No,' Sabatini said. 'I mean yes.'

'Sir?'

'Sorry. Coffee—long black, please. You, Cliff?'

'The same.'

As the waiter left I leaned across the table as if we had a secret: we didn't, just a question. 'What's behind it all, then? You make it sound like a conspiracy.'

'You said it, not me. That's why I'm talking to you and letting you buy me lunch. If Malouf's still alive and you can grab him, there're two possibilities.'

A guessing game, I thought. 'One is that if I can grab him we might find out what's going on. What's the other possibility?'

Sabatini stroked his beard. 'Malouf was one of the smartest hackers and cyber fraudsters we've seen. If he's alive he'd still be at it. This stuff's an addictive game for someone like him. All this might just be him! And remember, you said I'd get first bite.'

The person I most wanted to talk to next was Gretchen Nordlung but it wasn't the time. I went home. Sabatini had given me references to several other articles he'd written where he skirmished around the question of dodgy financial advisers and managers without getting himself into trouble. We have new libel laws allowing greater freedom for journalists, and judges are awarding lower damages than juries once did, but caution is still the keynote.

It was a familiar scene: I pulled up by my house and the door of a car parked on the opposite side of the street opened and the men who stepped out could only have been police. Not that they wore suits and hats; they favour leather jackets these days and a casual but clean look. Neat beards are in rather than moustaches. I stood by the front gate as they approached, the taller and older of the two showing his warrant card.

'Detective Sergeant Caulfield and DC Manning, Mr Hardy. We'd like a word with you.'

'What about?'

'Could we go inside?'

I looked up at the clear sky. 'Why? It's not raining.'

Caulfield sighed. 'They warned me about you. Here or at the station.'

'Could rain,' I said. 'Come on in.'

We went in and down the hall to the kitchen at the back where I set about making coffee. I spent a fair bit of money on the house a while back, but somehow its essential shabbiness had reasserted itself and it didn't look much different from what it was before the makeover.

Manning leaned back against the sink; Caulfield sat down at the breakfast nook and took out a notebook. The water boiled and I filled the glass jug and set the plunger.

'Black or white?'

'Nothing for us. What's your interest in Stefan Nordlung?'

'Who says I have one?'

'Photographs and footage taken by a bystander at the Spit marina where Nordlung was found dead this morning show you to have been present. You were also caught on a sweep shot taken by a TV news crew when they arrived. All this went to air on the midday news and one of our analysts identified you. So here we are, being nice.'

'Not very nice. You've refused my hospitality.'

Caulfield glanced at Manning. 'This is what they told us about, Ken. He wears you down with this sort of stuff until you lose your temper and do and say things you shouldn't. He's a past master at it, especially when he had a PEA licence, which he doesn't anymore.'

'Years of experience,' I said.

Caulfield closed his notebook and stood. He stacked up to about 185 centimetres, but I'm 188 and these days pushing 90 kilos. Not that it was going to get physical, not like in the days of DS 'Bumper' Flanagan, when physical was the name of the game. But it helps to stand your ground on an equal or better level.

'You're in our books, Hardy. First time we catch you putting your nose into police business you're in serious trouble. You're not licensed to do anything except pick your fucking nose. Any hint of harassment, a speeding violation, a nine thousand dollar deposit in a bank account, any sign of a gun and you're gone.'

'On what sort of charge?'

'Conspiracy's a big net with fine mesh. As witness the judge presently not getting out and about and having a jolly good time on his pension with his pals.'

I nodded. 'Terrorism'll stretch a bit, too.'

Caulfield glanced at Manning. 'That's a thought. All unnecessary if you tell us what you were doing there.'

'Maybe later,' I said. 'Leave me your card.'

Caulfield slapped a card down on the table and they trooped out, not slamming the door. This kind of thing had happened quite a few times since I'd lost my licence. I suppose the cops couldn't be blamed. There were always rogues in the profession; I wasn't the worst but, as Caulfield said, I had a habit of getting under police skins. For tough guys, police skins are thin.

I was upstairs at the computer, working through Sabatini's articles, when he rang.

'You didn't put all your cards on the table,' he said.

'How's that?'

'I saw the news. You were there when they fished Nordlung out.'

'Yes, I was just sticking to our no-names policy.'

'I'm not sure I buy that, but it's blown now. I bet I can guess who hired you.'

'Guess away.'

'Miles Standish, right?'

'Let's say you're right. How did you get there?'

'I'm not sure I can trust you. You're economical with the facts.'

I laughed. 'Nice one. Aren't we all? OK, well I'll give you something that might interest you. Two cops came to see me when I got home. Like you, they'd seen the news coverage and they warned me off. Obviously Nordlung meant something to them or why would they bother?'

There was a long pause and I thought I knew what was going through his head. I'd discussed this sort of thing with Lily a few times. Names, information, connections are the lifeblood of investigative journalism and private investigation alike. They're also the currency, to be hoarded or traded. Sabatini thought I'd hoarded a bit. He had something to trade, but was it worth his while? The other thing about information is that its value drops the more people share it. It has a use-by date. Sabatini made his decision.

'OK, you'd find out something about it sooner or later so you're getting it from me now: the real stuff. I'm investing in you, Hardy.'

I smiled. I'd read him correctly and he was even using the appropriate language. I didn't say anything.

'Nordlung and Standish were hand in glove. Standish brokered the deal that enabled Nordlung to buy the *Southern Star*. Are you with me?'

I was. The *Southern Star* was a cruise ship that was being fitted out for luxury voyages to the Antarctic. The work was being done in Hobart. The ship had exploded and was a total loss.

'Nordlung had it insured to the hilt and beyond,' Sabatini said. 'Massive premium. Standish raised the money and arranged the terms for that as well. Nordlung got a whacking great payout. If Nordlung's the one who's supposed to have seen Malouf you could be chasing shadows. Nordlung'd do anything Standish wanted him to.'

'So it wouldn't be in Standish's interest to kill him.'

'No; but there'd be plenty of candidates. Nordlung was a specialist in marine fraud of one kind or another. He started small and had some trouble, got bigger and honed his act. So are you investigating an alleged death or a real one, or both?'

'I wish I knew. Maybe nothing. Standish has made himself unavailable.'

'I could be wasting my time talking to you.'

'You could be.'

'I'm glad I did anyway. Know why?'

'Tell me.'

'Lily,' he said and hung up.

5

Common sense said to give it up as a bad job—too little substance, too many uncertainties, no focus. But common sense wouldn't pay the bills or help me out of the fix I was in with the option shares. That's if I really was in a fix. I'd been reading lately about fake emails, so I paid a call on Perry Hassan to make sure he had sent Standish the email I'd seen. We'd got together a few times since the Malouf scam and he'd been apologetic. He still was.

'I'm sorry, Cliff,' he said, 'but that's right. Dick Malouf had the management of the portfolio and that's what he did to you with those shares, probably just because he could. I know I was out of line telling Standish but he said he was thinking of employing you. I thought I was putting work your way.'

We were in his office in Five Dock, a large suite of rooms above a sprawling DVD rental joint. It used to be a relatively pleasant place to go the few times I went there—young, energetic accountants of both sexes working away in apparent open-plan harmony. Perry was a cynic who'd worked for the tax office in earlier days and was thought to know all the angles. He'd complained about executive lunches and desk-sitting piling on the kilos and I'd suggested he join my gym. He did and became an enthusiast. Now there was an air of despondency about the office and many fewer bodies.

'Well, you have, I think,' I said. 'What d'you make of Standish?'

'An operator. He put some people my way and then leaned on me to do certain favours. He says he's going to help me with the insurance people and I'm going to need all the help I can get. That's another reason why I gave him the details of your situation when he asked. Sorry.'

'It's all right. Is there any way to head off the margin call?'

Perry shrugged. 'A very good lawyer might be able to stall it for a while.'

'What about a conviction of Malouf for fraud?'

'He's dead.'

'Say he isn't.'

'Cliff, I'm up to my neck in lawyers, aggrieved clients and auditors. I can't sleep for worry. I can't find the will to go to the gym. I can't play games.'

'OK. One question: can Standish be trusted?'

He threw back his head and laughed. Then he looked

astonished and pleased that he was still able to laugh. So I'd
done him some good.

Like Perry, I hadn't been to the gym for a while. I decided
to have a workout and see if a spell on the treadmill gave me
any ideas. It's been known to happen. Late afternoon and
not many about. I stripped, stretched less thoroughly than I
should have, and started the treadmill at a brisk walk. If I felt
good I'd increase it to a trot. I was warmed up, considering
increasing the rate, when I heard a door crash and a shrill
voice cut through the *doof doof* musical fug.

'Where is that bastard? I'll kill him.'

I heard a crash of metal on metal and hit the off button.
A large man in a suit had picked up a short bar and slammed
it against one of the machines. A couple of people were doing
floor exercises on the mezzanine level. A man and a woman
leaned over the rail to look down. The intruder saw them and
rushed towards the stairs.

'You bastard, you cunt. I'll kill you both.'

He threw the short bar away. It clattered against a wall and
he picked up a longer, heavier one. That slowed him down
long enough for me to get between him and the stairs.

'Take it easy, mate.'

'Fuck you!'

He was big and strong and swung the bar with one hand,
but it wasn't made for swinging—too long, too heavy. The

movement put him off-balance. I grabbed the bar with both hands and twisted it out of his grasp. He roared and made a grab at me but I re-gripped and prodded him in the chest with the end of the bar and he stumbled and fell. I pinned him with the bar across his chest while Wesley, the gym manager and instructor, and two others came in to help. The would-be attacker glared up at us, swearing and spitting, but the fight went out of him.

We got him calmed down and convinced him that the two people he was after had left by the back exit.

'Just as well for you Cliff here stopped you,' Wesley said. 'You were on the way to assault with a deadly weapon grief.'

The man shrugged and brushed down his clothes. 'Who cares?'

He pushed us aside and made his way to the door.

'Cliff, my man, you've still got some moves,' Wesley said.

'He'd have done better with the short bar.'

'Don't even think it. I need a murder in here like I need swine flu. Haven't seen you for a while, man.'

'I've had some bad luck money-wise and other worries. In fact I'm probably going to be late paying my membership.'

Wesley laid his big dark hand on my shoulder. 'After what you did for me a while back, you've got a free pass as far as I'm concerned.'

I got back on the treadmill but my heart wasn't in it and I did the minimum amount of work on the machines and with the free weights. Although it was kind of Wesley to make the gesture (I'd got his son out of trouble a few years before), the idea of being a charity case didn't sit well with me. The Standish job, if it could be firmed up, gave me the prospect of recovering some money and earning some more. It was worth the effort, and I'd worked for less than honest people before.

I slept on it and decided that the first thing to do was get a stronger grip on Standish. I phoned the office but got nothing new from May Ling. I imagined her sitting there, able to cope with whatever came up, immaculate, carrying out her instructions to the letter.

In my experience, most separated wives keep pretty close tabs on their husbands for various reasons, some considerate, some not. I had a Vaucluse address for Felicity Standish.

I drove there in the usual sluggish traffic. The water to my left had a dull, gun-metal gleam under a heavy grey sky. Cars turned off New South Head Road towards Royal Sydney golf course, but I doubted that the players would get a full round in. What the Americans call a storm cell seemed to be building away to the east. I'm told they have leaf blowers on the tees and greens at Royal Sydney and people to immediately repair the fairway divots, but a flash of lightning and everyone heads for shelter just as at the roughest council course.

The Standish house was in a street that overlooked Nielsen Park out towards Shark Bay. Living there you were

41

gazing out from one millionaire's enclave across the water to another at Mosman.

The squattocracy that established the tone of Vaucluse included some honest men but not all, just as the present nabobs have some decent people among them. The address I had was a sandstone pile. There were pillars, a high wrought iron security gate and an electronic driveway gate in a high wall. Through the grille I could see a sweeping driveway and a fountain. It failed elegance, qualified as pretentious.

I buzzed at the gate.

'Yes.'

'I'd like to see Mrs Standish.'

'What about?'

'My name's Hardy. I was hired yesterday by Mr Standish to do a job. You could check on that by calling his office. I need to talk to him and I don't know where he is.'

'This is Felicity Standish. Are you saying Miles is missing?'

'I don't know. Maybe.'

'What does Rose Petal say?'

'Rose Petal?'

'May Ling.'

'She won't tell me anything. I'm not sure she knows where he is.'

'She knows. Have you got any ID?'

I held my cancelled PEA licence and driver's licence up to where I guessed the camera was.

'Thanks. Hang on, I'll make that call.'

I waited for no more than a minute before hearing a click and seeing the gate move a centimetre. I pushed and I was in. There was a two-car garage beside the house with a white Saab slotted in. A couple of colourful and expensive-looking children's tricycles occupied the other space. There were plastic toys around the fountain. So Standish was a family man. I'd never have guessed. Where was the profit?

I went up the wide steps to the front door, which opened at my approach. The woman who stood there was tall and slim, her figure displayed to best advantage in tight black jeans and a loose blue denim shirt. She wore ankle boots with medium heels and her dark hair and makeup had a perfect but unstudied look. She wasn't beautiful; she was almost plain, but she presented as if she were beautiful and it worked.

Her hand shot out and I took it. It was warm. The house would be warm inside so the shirt was adequate. She shook my hand and kept hold of it just long enough to make me feel as if I was being drawn inside.

'Come in, Mr Hardy. I've heard of you, of course. I believe we have things to talk about.'

She conducted me down a wide hallway past several doors on either side to a sitting room with a view out to a large garden and a swimming pool. The pool had a cover over it. Tall trees around the perimeter made the area totally private. There was a children's swing near the end of the yard and what looked like a cubby house in a tree. She waved to a chair.

'I've made coffee. Would you like some?'

'I would, thank you. Black, no sugar.'

She smiled and her face didn't look plain anymore. 'Of course. Just a minute.'

I stood and wandered around the room. The furniture was simple but expensive. A photograph of two children, a boy and girl, stood on top of a bookcase. A couple of paintings on the walls could have been originals and could have been good, but they were abstracts so how can you tell? Flowers in a vase were dropping their petals.

Felicity Standish came back in with two solid mugs. She handed me one. She invited me to sit and dropped down into one of the leather armchairs. I sat and tried the coffee. Hot and strong.

'You said you'd heard of me. From your husband?'

'Oh, no. Haven't seen him for weeks. No, I read the papers. I'm a crime junkie. Did you look at the books?'

I hadn't, but now I swivelled around to look. Crime novels and true crime—hardbacks and trade paperbacks.

'I read about you, and your partner being killed, and you losing your licence. You were in the news there for a while.'

I nodded. 'Unfortunately. I won't beat about the bush, Mrs Standish. I was hired to look for Richard Malouf.'

Her hands tightened around the coffee mug. 'He's dead.'

'He may not be.'

'I'd know if he were alive; he was my lover. Oh, but I can see you already knew that. Miles told you. Hated to do it, but he did, right?'

I nodded.

'Did he tell you that he was screwing his secretary? No? But you're not surprised. Well, you wouldn't be—she's very beautiful and with a heart like a block of ice.'

I drank the coffee while she told me that after she became aware of Standish's infidelity she was easy meat for Malouf, who caught her in a down cycle and lifted her out of it. For a while.

'I don't know why I'm telling you all this,' she said. 'I don't know you.'

'I've got a trustworthy face.'

Her laugh was an embarrassed snort. 'I wouldn't say that, but I would say it isn't judgemental.'

'Thank you.'

'But you're being led up the garden path, Mr Hardy. You see, I think Miles Standish had Richard Malouf murdered.'

6

'That surprised you, didn't it?' Felicity Standish said.

I said, 'Yes. Are you serious?'

'I'm deadly serious. Although Miles was a serial adulterer, he couldn't handle it when I made one misstep. He can't bear to lose anything. That's why he's creating so much difficulty about our divorce.'

I looked around the room and out to the garden. 'Well, it's a lot to give up.'

She laughed. 'No, no, this is all mine. I inherited it. I put that badly. What I mean is that he can't bear not to win. He was good at a whole range of sports and his legal studies and at business. He married a rich woman and has a son and a daughter. A winner all the way until this happened. He was ruthless at everything, swept opposition aside. He beat up a man I was seeing before we got together. He had some cause, but it cost him money to avoid an assault charge. I think he was capable of killing Richard or having it done. He was certainly a police suspect, probably still is.'

The implication of what she was saying was clear. Maybe Standish had hired me to divert attention away from him, to muddy the waters. Felicity Standish drank the last of her coffee and sat, looking composed. I thought about the shelf of books and wondered whether she had overstimulated her imagination. I still had enough police contacts to establish whether Standish was a suspect in Malouf's death, but I urgently needed to talk to Standish, otherwise I was stumbling around in the dark.

'Where are the kids?' I said.

'At school. Why?'

'Does your husband have access, visiting rights, picking up arrangements?'

'Hah, I see where you're going. He has those rights but he hasn't exercised them for weeks. You need to contact him and I need to know where he is. How about I hire you to find him?'

I shook my head.

'Why not? Not ethical? You're de-licensed. You couldn't have a contract with Miles and you don't need one with me. What d'you say?'

'No, too much conflict of interest. I need to find him for my own reasons.'

'Fair enough, but the offer remains open. I'll give you the clue I would've given you if you'd accepted. If you want to find Miles Standish, keep tabs on May Ling. That shouldn't be too hard for a man like you. Should be a pleasure.'

The storm swept in and dumped water on the city and then departed as if satisfied. The sun shone through a thin cloud cover but a wind kept the temperature low. I did some scouting. A lane runs behind the buildings that front New South Head Road in Edgecliff. At the end of the lane was a small, undercover car park, electronically controlled. The only alternative all-day parking for anyone working in the area was the huge, multi-level operation on the opposite side of the road over the railway station. Somehow I didn't think May Ling was the type to battle with the plebs in the concrete jungle. That's where I put my car while I had a slow lunch in a restaurant nearby, read the morning paper from cover to cover and took a one-hour walk up to Darling Point and back.

At four forty-five I was sitting in my car in the lane where parking was illegal and keeping my eye out for inspectors. Eventually they'll install cameras in these places, sack the inspectors and reap greater rewards, but just for now human beings were still useful. The afternoon had turned cold; parking inspectors are like everyone else— given the choice they'll do their job in greater comfort and there were ample opportunities to work under cover along the main road.

At five fifteen May Ling came tripping down the lane. She had a minimalist silver-grey umbrella up against the drizzle and despite her high heels she avoided puddles like a dancer obeying a choreographer to perfection. She wore a grey suit with an unfastened silvery rain slicker over it and her face seemed to glow in the damp, shaded surroundings. She closed the umbrella as she entered the car park and one hand dipped into her grey suede shoulder bag. When it came to accessories, May Ling was right there.

After five minutes, a silver Peugeot slid out of the car park. French, it figured. The car headed towards the city and I fell in behind it, keeping two cars back. The evening was drawing in and headlights, brake lights and indicators were sharp in the gloom. May Ling was a precise, cautious driver. She signalled her intentions early and was easy to follow. She entered the tunnel, was patient as the lanes clogged up and didn't try any fancy moves although other cars were jostling for position. This was a woman in control of herself and not letting anything disturb her composure.

The hazard of following anyone in these conditions is in the prospect of them stopping. If the quarry pulls in and stops and there's no parking space close by, you're gone. You have to move on and your chance of circling round and taking another couple of passes is almost nil. May Ling didn't stop. She went on to North Sydney, took a left and worked her way

back to McMahons Point and the water. I wasn't familiar
with the area, but it looked like the kind of place where May
Ling and the silver Peugeot would fit right in.

She pulled up outside a block of flats as a light rain fell.
I went further up the street, parked and watched. She turned
on the interior light and used her mobile phone. A couple of
minutes later a man came hurrying from the block. He wore
a raincoat with the hood up, completely concealing his face.
He looked to be about the same size as Standish and moved
like a fit man, but I couldn't be sure. May Ling had turned
out the light after the phone call, so I couldn't see anything
inside her car once he got in. She started the engine and
drove off in her steady, careful way.

Thursday night and busy. I followed the car back to North
Sydney. May Ling cruised, looking for a parking spot, and
found one. I had to park illegally to keep in touch. I'd get
a ticket, but I was on expenses. Or was I? I didn't have a
raincoat and I got wet following the pair along the street
with only occasional cover from the awnings. The man kept
his hood up. They walked close together but didn't touch.
They entered a Chinese restaurant doing a roaring trade, but
they must have made a booking because they were seated
straight off.

'Sir?'

The head waiter looked sceptically at my jeans, windcheater and damp leather jacket.

'Can I wait at the bar for a free table?'

'Are you alone, sir?'

When I hear that I always want to come out with the Jake Gittes line: 'Aren't we all?' but I restrained myself. I said I had a friend coming.

'There could be a table for two in about thirty minutes. By all means wait in the bar.'

'Pencil me in,' I said.

He smiled, unamused.

I sat at the bar and ordered a glass of the house red. It cost ten dollars and the woman behind the bar poured it precisely so that you couldn't complain that it was too little, but certainly couldn't feel that it was generous. I had a clear view now of May Ling and her companion, who was definitely Standish but not the man I'd been with two days ago. He appeared pale and as if he'd lost weight. He had what looked like a double whisky in front of him and he was working on it as if it was his last drink in this life. May Ling slipped her jacket off in the warm room. Her pale neck was swan-like; her breasts suggested picture-perfection under her silk blouse. She had her hand on Standish's arm with the slender fingers moving gently but it wasn't doing him any good. The man was clearly close to his emotional limit.

After a while, say two-thirds of my glass of wine, Standish and May Ling were joined by two Chinese men. Both were medium-size, well dressed and known to the head waiter, who almost bowed to the floor on greeting them. Two chairs were quickly pulled out to allow them to sit down with a minimum of effort. They accepted all this as their right. They would.

I knew both of the men and the face of one had been in the newspapers and on television. The older of the two, the one with grey in his hair, was Freddy Wong. Freddy had avoided gaol for more than twenty years. He'd been acquitted several times—of drug importation, home invasion and conspiracy to commit murder, twice. The other man was his brother. No wonder Standish looked stressed.

I'd come up against Freddy Wong about ten years earlier when helping a Chinese family rescue a girl from a brothel he'd controlled. It was the classical thing—an offer of domestic employment, the arrangement of a visa and then the trap closed. But Wong or his agent had miscalculated. The girl had family in Sydney, including a police officer. They hired me and I worked with the cop to get the girl and several other women away and recover their passports. It had involved a violent confrontation between me and Wong's lieutenant—his brother. Threats were issued but nothing came of it.

Standish's involvement with the Wong brothers put a whole new spin on things. Added to that, Freddy Wong was one of the gamblers Malouf was said to have lost money to.

7

The Wongs had their backs to me but I still kept my head low and a hand up to my face. I searched my memory for Freddy's brother's name without a result. I remembered his snarling aggression and the fight we'd had in a lane behind the brothel in Petersham. It wasn't a martial arts affair, nothing balletic, just a knock-down, drag-out fist fight. He was fast and strong but he didn't have the timing and technique you need for that sort of stoush. We fought at close quarters, between two garbage skips, and there was no space for bullocking rushes, which would have been his preferred style. He swung a lot and missed a lot. A straight punch beats a swing most times, cumulatively. I wore him down and left him dazed and bleeding in the gutter.

Lester, that was it. It was all coming back to me. The Wong brothers weren't refugees or asylum seekers. The family had been here since the gold rushes, and members had prospered as merchants and professionals—but they'd formed links with the criminal element in the more recent arrivals and had their fingers in all the pies. Freddy had been to Fort Street High School and Sydney University for a medical degree. He'd never worked as a doctor. Lester had never worked at anything except as Freddy's muscle. The two men bore no physical resemblance: Freddy was squat and fat, verging on obese; Lester was medium tall and lean. He'd been a speed addict and his couple of brief gaol terms—for assault and wounding—were unlikely to have rehabilitated or detoxified him.

Things weren't going well at the table. Freddy Wong was shaking his head emphatically while Lester tucked in to the food. Then a man who fitted the generic description 'of Middle Eastern appearance' joined them and the discussion got heated. May Ling looked anxious as she tried to soothe all the players. Standish had completely lost his appetite.

It wasn't the time to intrude, especially in those surroundings where the Wongs were likely to have useful supporters. I finished my drink and moved away from the bar.

'Sir,' the head waiter said, 'a table is being cleared for you.'

'I've been stood up.'

'What a shame. Perhaps you'll come again.'

I drove home thinking that the evening hadn't been a complete waste of time; it had thrown up a lot of questions.

What exactly was the relationship between Standish and May Ling? Why had he dropped out of sight, and what was he doing playing chopsticks with the Wong brothers? May Ling had to be the go-between, but what kind of deal was she brokering? And what of the Middle Eastern wild card?

I called in on Megan and Hank and ate their leftover shepherd's pie. They were still feeling the glow of approaching parenthood and I didn't want to dim it by talking about my concerns. Hank said his parents would be coming out for the birth. Megan's mother, my ex-wife Cyn, was dead. The kid would be down one grandparent and it'd be up to me to do a good job in the solo role.

'Have you ever actually held a baby in your arms, Cliff?' Megan asked.

'Sure, my sister's kids.'

'Boys or girls?'

'Um . . .'

Hank laughed. 'We've all gotta lot to learn. What're you doing with yourself, Cliff?'

I hadn't told them about my financial reverses. 'Managing my financial affairs,' I said, which was true in a way.

I left them still happy, and some of that rubbed off on me as it had before and as I hoped it would again. As I drove home I had to search my memory again for the name of the Chinese policeman I'd worked with on the matter of Freddy Wong's sex slaves. It didn't come to me until I was half asleep after five pages of a recent Miles Franklin Award-winning novel I'd bought as a remainder—Stephen Chang.

Frank Parker was a long-time friend who'd retired as a deputy police commissioner but remained on their books as a consultant. He had access to police databases closed to civilians. With the previous night's damp clothes in the dryer, I rang him early, knowing that he'd soon be off cycling or playing squash or swimming laps. I'd put on some weight recently, and Frank's trim figure was a constant reproach.

'Frank, it's Cliff.'

'Gidday, Cliff, feel like a swim?'

'Ask me round about December. No, I need some help locating a member of the New South Wales police service.'

'Oh, Jesus, you're not working, are you? You've got no standing, mate, no protection. One bad move and they'll chop you off at the knees. You know that.'

'Yeah, I know, but this is a personal matter.'

'It's always personal with you. I'm not going to help you talk your way into court and gaol . . . again.'

'Hey, did I tell you I'm going to be a grandfather?'

'No. What? When? Hey, Hilde, Megan's pregnant.'

He was talking to his wife, Hilde Stoner, who'd been a tenant of mine when I was battling to meet the mortgage after Cyn had flown the coop. I'd introduced them. I could hear a squeal from Hilde (the Parkers had grandchildren, twins, they were devoted to). Then Frank came back on the line.

'You're working me, you bastard. OK, what is it?'

'I need to get in touch with Stephen Chang, you remember, we—'

'I remember. Shit, the Wong brothers. Don't tell me you're going down that road again.'

'Obliquely,' I said. 'Can you get me a number?'

I could hear Hilde asking for more details about the prospective Hardy grandchild and Frank fending her off. His voice when he came back was full of resignation.

'Hilde says congratulations. Me too. I'll put you on to Steve Chang only because I know he's sensible enough not to have anything to do with you. When're we going to see you?'

'Soon.'

'Yeah. I'll text you, Cliff.'

The text came through soon after I took the clothes out of the dryer. The jeans were tight around the waist. I had to get back to the gym more often, charity case or not. Sucking in the love handles, zipping up, I rang the number Frank had given me.

'Chang.'

Like the Wongs, Stephen Chang's forebears had been in Australia longer than some of mine. His accent was pure Sydney.

'This is Cliff Hardy. I don't know what to call you these days. I'm betting you're not just a senior constable anymore.'

'Detective Inspector. It's been a long time. What can I do for you, Mr Hardy?'

It used to be Cliff, but he'd gone up and I'd gone down and he was being careful.

'I'm dealing with something involving our old friends the Wong brothers. I thought you might be able to help me.'

'How do you mean *dealing*? I understood you were retired.'

'It's a long story. Could we meet? What's your role these days?'

'I'm heading up a unit looking into Asian crime and certain links.'

There'd been a spate of home invasions recently. One had resulted in the death of an elderly couple and in another, a policeman called to the scene had been left in a coma by the attackers. He wasn't expected to recover and the affair had caused a lot of law and order activity among the politicians. It didn't surprise me that a task force had been appointed.

'Home invasion, you mean? Drugs? Freddy Wong was into home invasion ten years back,' I said.

'So he was—a sideline of his. It's a bit broader than that. I suppose we could have a talk. Are you still in Glebe?'

I said I was and we arranged to meet in the coffee bar next to the old Valhalla theatre, now defunct and awaiting its fate. It was a few minutes walk away for me. I knew that the number I'd rung was the Surry Hills police centre. Chang gave himself an hour to get there. Friday traffic.

Anti-discrimination laws put an end to the police imposing a minimum height requirement for recruits. This allowed quite a few Asians to join who were previously excluded. Didn't apply to Stephen Chang; he stood 190 centimetres and had played basketball at university. He'd made pretty good time and I was only hanging around briefly before he showed up. Smart suit, overcoat, no tie. A lot of grey in his hair, although he couldn't have been more than thirty-five. We shook hands and took seats at an outside table. I turned the collar of my jacket up against the cold.

'So,' Chang said, 'you don't look so bad for someone who's lost his licence and had a heart attack.'

'I'm OK. You look . . . authoritative. Coffee?'

We ordered and I gave him an outline of how the man who'd hired me to investigate an alleged death had named as a witness someone who'd been murdered the very next day, gone into hiding and emerged to meet with Freddy and Lester Wong and hadn't looked happy. His level of interest lifted sharply when I mentioned the man who had joined the group and provoked discord.

'Lebanese?'

I shrugged. 'Could be.'

'This is interesting. You haven't told me the name of your client and I'm not surprised because you're not supposed to have any bloody clients. Who was murdered?'

I don't know what it was: my lack of status, my health, my financial situation, my approaching grandfatherhood, but I was acutely aware that I needed help. 'Stefan Nordlung,' I said.

Chang almost choked on the dregs of his flat white. 'Christ almighty, Hardy. Do you have any idea what you've got yourself into?'

8

Chang told me that part of his brief was to investigate links between Asian and Lebanese criminals and that marine insurance scams were one of the areas of concern, along with drugs, people smuggling and extortion.

'What's the name of your task force?'

Chang smiled. 'It's a serious investigative unit, so it doesn't have a silly name. The people we're interested in launder drug and extortion money by buying boats, insuring them, scuppering them and collecting the insurance. Then they collect on the salvage. Sometimes they rehabilitate the boat altogether and go through the process again. They have people inside the insurance companies playing along, also some inside finance companies. It's complex, with all sorts of legal and accounting tangles.'

I said I knew Nordlung had been involved in a dodgy insurance deal. 'But he isn't Asian or Lebanese.'

'His wife's Chinese.'

'Her name's Gretchen.'

'She changed it. We think Nordlung was up to his balls and beyond in this stuff. Something must've gone wrong and he paid a price. He wasn't the only one. These people don't hesitate to clean a slate. How did you know about Nordlung?'

I produced DS Caulfield's card. 'He told me. I assume you're working together on this?'

Chang smiled. 'How much do you know about police politics?'

I knew a fair bit from personal experience and talking with Frank Parker over the years. The old antagonism between the 'kneelers' and the 'shakers'—the Catholics and the Masons—had given way to divisions over the roles of specialised units and the personalities of senior officers. With a bit of intra-state and federal/state rivalry thrown in. I watched Chang push the card away.

'Not a team?' I said.

'Not exactly. Caulfield's Serious Crimes. They're not enamoured with a unit headed up by a slope with a Muslim 2IC. These are murky waters you've got into, Cliff.'

So I was Cliff again. 'Caulfield warned me off. Are you doing the same?'

'No, I'm thinking you could be very useful.'

* * *

After all the years I'd spent in the investigation business I thought I'd seen and experienced just about everything, but Chang's proposition was something new.

'You want me to act as an undercover cop?'

'Something like that, yes.'

'Why would I do that?'

'Why not? Are you telling me you've never pretended to be something you weren't before?'

'Of course not, but . . .'

'But what?'

I hadn't identified my client (if that was the word), but it wouldn't have taken Chang long to work it out. A quick call to Caulfield would do the trick whether they were simpatico or not. Although everything was getting tricky I still felt some provisional loyalty towards Standish until I could be convinced he didn't deserve it. I thought about how desperate he'd looked in the restaurant and how little effect May Ling's solicitude was having. Given her allure that was true desperation.

'I've got an obligation.'

'Of course you have, but you've already told me that the man you have an obligation to didn't look comfortable with the Wongs and the Middle Easterner—let's call him a Lebanese. I'm telling you that if your man is involved with the Asian/Lebo connection the best way you could help him would be to help get some of those bastards into court.'

'And get myself targeted by the others?'

'Come on, what else are you going to do—just drop it?'

It was a good question. I hate loose ends and, as things stood, there were more loose ends than anything else. Quite apart from any duty to Standish there was the question of Richard Malouf. Was he alive or was he dead? I couldn't just let it go.

'I can give you phone numbers so that you can get me or Karim Ali, my number two, at any time twenty-four seven. And a number that can get you backup very, very quickly. As far as humanly possible, we'll see your guy right for as long as you want. What d'you say?'

I nodded agreement. Chang took out his mobile.

'What're you doing?' I said.

'Just hang on.' He made a call and spoke briefly before closing the phone. 'I've got a couple of people watching us just in case there's someone watching you.'

'I checked that for myself before you got here.'

'Glad to hear it. Just making sure. All clear, then. Thanks for the coffee. We'll keep in touch.'

He unwound his long frame and strolled away. Good exit line—I liked that 'we'.

Strange though the circumstances were, I decided to proceed as I would have in a normal investigation and that meant little more than following my instincts. I now knew where Standish was and, more or less, how to get in touch with him. There were only half a dozen flats in the McMahons Point block and I felt pretty sure I could bluff my way to the right one. Eventually I'd have to confront Standish and convince him he needed my help, but for the moment I was still intrigued by the initial question about Malouf. His wife had ID'd him: if he was still alive she'd lied.

The address I had for Rosemary Malouf was in Bondi Junction. I phoned and learned that it was a travel agency. The man I spoke to said she was on her morning tea break. I made an appointment to see Mrs Malouf straight after her lunch break at two pm. I still had the card Malouf had given me at one of our brief meetings and I thought I could use it to get her attention at least long enough for me to make an assessment of her. I fitted in a gym session before driving there and even had time to have a look at the beach. I skipped lunch.

The travel agency was a hole-in-the-wall kind of place with the usual array of glossy posters and advertisements for airlines and package tours. Tourism is down, they say, and this place certainly seemed to bear that out. I was the only person to go in and the smile on the face of the young man seated behind the desk faded when I told him why I was there.

'Rose'll be back any minute. Then I can get away for a job interview, thank God.'

'Things are slow?'

'Non-existent. Here she is.'

A woman stepped into the office, taking off her coat. She was thirtyish, small, and pretty in a fair, fragile sort of way. 'Off you go, Troy. Good luck. Good afternoon, Mr Hardy.'

Troy grabbed a coat and hurried out as I sat on the other side of Rosemary Malouf's desk. 'Now what can I do for you? Troy said you were a bit mysterious on the phone. Are you planning a trip?'

I shook my head and put Malouf's card down on the desk. Her neat little jaw tightened as she looked at it.

'What d'you want?' she said. 'I haven't got any money.'

'He has.'

'He gambled it all away and then he was killed. Please leave.'

'You identified him.'

'Yes.'

'Someone claims to have seen him alive.'

'Go away.' She reached into her bag for her mobile phone. 'I'm calling the police.'

'I'm working with the police.'

A look of sheer terror came into her face. She dropped the phone and buried her face in her hands. 'Go away. Go away, please.'

There was nothing else to do. She kept her face covered and her hands were shaking. I picked up Malouf's card and replaced it with one of my own. It was long out of date in describing me as a PEA, but at least it had my contact details minus the office number.

'I'm sorry to distress you,' I said. 'You can contact me if you need any help.'

She shook her head, keeping it low, and began punching numbers on her mobile. I left the shop and went to a coffee place on the other side of the street. I sat inside by the window and had a clear view of the travel agency as I worked on a watery flat white. Troy came back looking depressed. It was a miserable moment for everyone.

After about thirty minutes a car pulled up outside the travel agency. It parked illegally, but neither the driver nor the man who got out of the back seat seemed to care. He went into the shop. I paid for my coffee and took up a position where I could get a good view of whoever left the shop but couldn't be easily seen myself. I had a state of the art mobile phone Megan had bought me. I hadn't mastered all its functions but I knew enough to enable me to zoom and get a good set of pictures.

I had the camera to the ready when the man came out of the shop and I caught him as he moved towards the car. He stopped and lit a cigarette before he got in. He was stocky and dark, wearing a well-cut suit and an unbuttoned, double-breasted overcoat. I recognised him: he was the man who'd joined the Wong brothers, May Ling and Miles Standish in the North Sydney Chinese restaurant.

9

I downloaded the photographs onto my computer and sent them as an attachment in an email to Chang, asking him if he could identify the man. Chang phoned me almost immediately.

'I'm sending someone to see you,' he said.

'Really? Why?'

'He'll explain.'

'Come on, Stephen. Who are we talking about?'

'My 2IC, Karim Ali.'

'You know what I mean. Who's the bloke in the photos I sent?'

'It's not something to talk about over the phone.'

'Give me the name or I won't be here when your guy calls.'

'He's Selim Houli. You don't want to know him. Watch out for Karim, he'll be there soon.'

He hung up. I went to my notebook and saw the name I'd transcribed from Standish's list: Selim Houli was one of the gamblers who was said to have taken serious money from Malouf. According to Standish's notes, his club was the Tiberias in Darlinghurst Road. I Googled it while waiting for Chang's offsider.

The website for the Tiberias Club featured audio and video on its attractions. Its cocktail bar was a shimmering light show with barmaids in fishnets, g-strings and nipple pasties serving customers wearing expensive clothes and jewellery and having a wonderful time.

There was a small dance floor with no more than twenty tables arranged around it in front of a small stage. A button click brought the scene to life with jazzy music playing and three men and three women performing a routine that stopped just this side of actual sexual activity in all its many and varied forms. It was only a brief sound and movement bite, but it was skilfully shot with effective lighting and the performers were top class. An expert, expensive, erotic production.

Static again, the site provided details on provisional and actual membership, the club's privacy policy, restrictions on photographic and recording devices and strict rules about insobriety. The floor show must have been on a loop, because it came on again without me activating it just as I heard the doorbell ring downstairs.

I went to the door, looked through the peephole, and saw

a dark-faced young man with a serious expression. I opened the door.

I've been hit quite a few times in quite a few places, but the blow that came at me then was faster and more surprising than anything I've experienced. It drove the wind out of me, collapsed me at the knees, and seemed to blind me, all in an instant. Then time slowed down. One second I was standing and conscious and the next I was floating towards the floor. I tried to throw out my arms to shield myself against the fall but I couldn't move them. I didn't even feel the bump.

When I came out of the fog I was sitting in a chair in what I sensed rather than saw was a darkened room, with plastic restraints around my wrists. I could hear something disturbing the air but couldn't make out what. It was as though my senses had all been diminished; I couldn't see, hear or smell properly.

It's said that 'Gentleman' Jim Corbett was paralysed by Bob Fitzsimmons's punch that robbed him of his world heavyweight title. I'd never believed it but I did now. A kind of paralysis had made me useless back in the doorway of my house and something similar, but even more debilitating, was happening now. *What's that noise? What's that smell? Why can't I see?*

A light came on and I lifted my hands to shield my eyes from it. At least I could move and close my eyes. The noise stopped and I realised it had been music, coming from not so very far off. The light swung away and I opened my eyes. A man I recognised as Selim Houli was sitting opposite me about a metre away. He was smoking a cigar.

'Mr Hardy,' he said. 'How do you feel?'

I was in my shirtsleeves and I tried to scratch at my upper left arm where I felt a pain, but the restraints stopped me.

'Yes,' Houli said. 'A small injection to tranquillise you.'

For a second I wondered whether I still had the power of speech. As it came out my voice was a raw croak. 'I can put that on the list of the laws you've broken.'

He laughed and expelled aromatic smoke. 'Oh, that's a very long list indeed, depending on your point of view.'

I said nothing and concentrated on getting myself back together. Houli was obviously someone who liked to talk and talkers often do themselves much more harm than good. As my vision cleared I looked around the room. It was a sort of storage space with boxes and furniture stacked up. The two chairs we were sitting on had clearly been brought in for the purpose. I had a sense of it being below ground level. Nothing social went on down here normally.

Houli looked to be in his forties with thinning dark hair and a five o'clock shadow. He wore the suit I'd seen him in earlier at Bondi Junction with the jacket unbuttoned. White business shirt, discreetly striped silk tie, gold watch and a gold half-crown on one of his front teeth. He was olive-skinned with dark patches under his eyes. He flicked ash from the cigar onto the cement floor.

'You told Rosemary Malouf that you believed her husband was still alive.'

'Did I?'

'Don't be foolish, Mr Hardy. You're in a very dangerous position. I urge you to cooperate.'

'I'll do my best.'

'Have you seen Richard Malouf?'

I didn't answer.

'Have you spoken to anyone who *has* seen him?'

Not the best interrogative technique, showing that you want something quite badly. Unfortunately I had nothing to bargain with, except silence.

Houli sighed. He dropped his cigar to the floor and stepped on it. 'I can't tell whether that means yes or no. I need you to make it clear to me. How would you like to meet Yusef again?'

'If he's the guy who hit me, I would.' I held up my hands. 'Without these.'

'No.' He got up, crossed to the door and rapped on it. It opened and the young serious face I'd seen through the peephole was looking at me again. He wore jeans, work boots and a T-shirt with the short sleeves fully filled by biceps and triceps. Houli nodded to him and he walked over towards me. I started to stand but he kicked me in both shins—right boot to left shin, left boot to right shin.

The pain shot up my legs. A soccer player. I sat down hard.

'It's very simple for you,' Houli said. 'I asked you two questions and you will answer. You are a small man, Mr Hardy, and you have become involved in something much too big for you. I made it my business to find out a little about you. You've had some successes and some failures, would you agree?'

'Who hasn't?'

'I haven't had any failures and I don't intend to start having them.'

'Good luck.'

'Luck has nothing to do with it, but you're right if I understand you correctly. I am under a certain amount of pressure which is why you are under pressure now.'

I began to revise my opinion of him. He was a talker, but he was also intelligent and very dangerous. By admitting that he was under pressure he'd upped the wattage on his threat to me. People behave according to what's at stake and for Houli it was clearly something big.

I said nothing but closed my eyes as a wave of nausea hit me.

The leg pain warred for dominance with the deep ache higher up where Yusef had first hit me. The vile taste flooding my senses made me angry, not compliant. I ignored Yusef and stared at Houli thinking how much I'd like to displace his gold tooth. A blow to the left side of my face was followed by one to the other side. A searing pain went through my head and I was sure that an eardrum had broken, maybe both. I called them every obscene name I could think of and tried to stop my head from drooping.

Yusef hit me again several times and I kept my mouth shut. I could feel blood dripping somewhere. A low blow had me retching. I heard a click and saw Houli lighting a cigar and blowing on the tip to make it glow brightly. He moved closer and Yusef ripped my shirt open and then stepped back.

'Shit,' he said, 'he's had a heart operation. Any more could kill him, like—'

'Shut up,' Houli snapped. 'But you're right, we don't want that.' He puffed on the cigar, looked at it and shook his head. 'I don't think he knows anything useful anyway. He's just a dumb stubborn arsehole blundering about. Give him a jab, load him up with something, and dump him.'

They left the room and Yusef came back quickly with a plastic syringe in his hand. I tried to fend him off but he was too quick for me and I felt the needle sink into my upper arm. The room started to swirl around me and I heard myself giggling. Yusef hauled me up and dragged me across the room. I struggled, still laughing; my head hit the door and I blacked out.

I was staggering through an amusement park full of flashing lights and jangly music with the sounds of horns honking and people shouting and with the ground slipping sideways under my feet. I almost fell but got myself upright and lurched on. Something large, smelly and noisy brushed by me and I laughed at it and aimed a kick but it had gone. Then there were more people with pale, blurry faces and angry teeth. They parted in front of me, peeled off, and I felt as if I was riding a surfboard with the waves buffeting me, threatening my balance.

I bounced off something hard and then again off something soft. My head hurt. One ear felt as though a siren was blowing in it full bore. I put my hand up to it, but the noise just got louder and I started to swear and stagger as the pain hit me. I was cold; my chest was bare; I could feel a chill wind biting into me, and my shirt felt like a flapping rag.

Two figures loomed up in front of me and didn't move. Big things, blue things with hats. The hats looked funny and I laughed.

I said, 'Funny hats,' and swung a punch at one of the hats. I missed, lost balance and collapsed into what felt like a warm, hard embrace.

10

I didn't want to say it, but there was nothing else to say. 'Where am I?'

The woman in the white dress and cap and blue cardigan said, 'You're in St Vincent's Hospital, Mr . . .' she consulted her clipboard, '. . . Hardy.'

'How did I get here?'

'The police brought you in. Apparently you assaulted one of them, although how you could given the condition you were in is beyond me.'

My head throbbed and my body ached. 'What is my condition?'

She looked at the notes again. 'You have a perforated eardrum and multiple bruises and lacerations, some of them requiring stitches. There was some concern that your spleen might have been ruptured but that's uncertain at this point. Your blood pressure is very high.'

'I'm on medication for that but I haven't taken it for . . .' I felt my stubble. 'How long have I been here?'

'Thirty-six hours, give or take. There were various drugs in your system that had to be monitored. You were close to comatose when you were brought in. The doctors will be surprised at the speed of your recovery. *Don't* try to sit up!'

My attempt didn't amount to much and I was happy to settle back on the pillows. I was in a small room with the usual hospital fittings. A television set was mounted on the wall at an inconvenient angle and elevation. There was a cannula in my right hand, a drip hanging from a stand beside the bed. It all reminded me of when I'd had the bypass, but with fewer tubes in and out.

A young doctor came in and looked at the notes. He needed a shave and his eyes were red and tired-looking. 'Doctor Rasamussen,' he said. 'Hello.'

I said hello and watched him. His white coat was crumpled and his shirt was a long way from fresh. He and the nurse took some blood, checked my blood pressure and temperature.

'How does the ear feel?' the doctor said.

'Sore.'

'It will be. It's been damaged externally and internally. Have to see what can be done there. But you're in better shape than I'd have expected, Mr Hardy. You're very resilient, I'd say.'

I nodded. 'I've always healed quickly.'

'I believe you. You've been knocked about a bit over the years, haven't you?'

'Recreational and professional wear and tear.'

'Interesting. As what?'

'Boxer, soldier, private investigator.'

'Really. Well there's a policeman anxious to see you. Are you up to it?'

I said I was. The doctor and the nurse left and Stephen Chang strolled in.

'No grapes?' I said.

'No fucking grapes. Jesus, Hardy, you're a walking disaster.'

He told me that I'd been found wandering in Kings Cross in a disoriented condition, laughing and shouting, and that I'd taken a swing at a cop before collapsing into his arms. They'd taken me to the station where they'd found a couple of ecstasy tablets and a small amount of cocaine in my pockets.

'They also found this.' Chang produced a crumpled card from his pocket. 'My card. They rang me and here you are.'

'Thank you.'

'What happened?'

I told him what I could remember of it. There were blank spots and places where I couldn't tell whether something had actually happened or I'd imagined it.

He didn't do sympathy. 'Couldn't tell one Lebo from another, eh?'

'I didn't know what your man looked like.'

'He'd have held his warrant card up at the peephole.'

'Okay. I was careless. My guard was down.'

'It could be that you're past it. So it was Selim Houli and from your description it sounds like it was a bastard called Yusef Talat that took you. And Houli wanted to know if you'd seen Richard Malouf?'

I nodded and wished I hadn't. Everything above the neck hurt and I wondered about the hospital's policy on painkillers. I reckoned that I could do with something pretty heavy.

'That's right,' I said. 'So it all comes back to that. Is Malouf alive or not? And why does it matter to so many people?'

'No idea,' Chang said. 'What's wrong?'

Sweat had broken out all over my body and I was shivering. Chang's face blew up like a balloon and when he stood he looked to be three metres tall. I heard him call for a nurse and then there was a bustle of bodies and voices and I could make no sense of it at all.

When I came out of the warm mist Megan and Hank were there, looking relieved. They told me that I'd had a bad reaction to one of the drugs I'd been given and had gone into a coma for a day or so.

'Dangerous places, hospitals,' I said. 'Remind me to stay out of them in future.'

'What the hell were you doing to take a beating like

that?' Megan said. She was beginning to show signs of the pregnancy and I couldn't help smiling at the sight.

'Don't smile,' she said. 'You're supposed to be retired.'

I filled them in as best I could, skipping bits here and there, admitting that I was close to broke and facing a worrying debt.

Megan said, 'I hope you've kept your medical insurance up.'

I nodded. 'I trust you're well covered. How's it coming along?'

She couldn't help smiling herself now. 'Perfectly.'

'Are you going to need any help, Cliff?' Hank said.

Megan glared at him. 'You're not going on with it after this, are you?'

'I have to, love, but not for a while. I've got the police onside for a change, and if I need help, Hank, I'll ask.'

She wasn't happy, but, stubborn as she was, she knew I was the same. They undertook to collect the mail at my house, to visit and to help me get home. I slept a bit, ate and drank a bit, managed to shuffle along to the toilet taking my drip stand with me, and felt improvement hour by hour.

The drip had gone and my mind was clear and my body less aching when Chang appeared again. He was accompanied by a small dark man, immaculately dressed, who he introduced as Detective Sergeant Karim Ali.

'You had me worried,' Chang said.

'I'm OK, a minor glitch. I know what you're going to say—nothing to be done about Houli. No evidence.'

'That's right.'

'Who's this Talat character?'

Ali shrugged. I could tell at once that he didn't like me—some cops do, most don't. 'Muscle, ex-militia.'

'He's good at what he does. I'm wondering if he was involved in Nordlung's death. Nordlung looked to be a pretty big guy. Yachtsmen are strong. Someone must have subdued him efficiently and quietly before putting him into the water.'

Ali said, 'It's possible. He's got all the skills—frogman, paratrooper, explosives expert.'

'Shit,' I said, 'how'd he get in?'

Ali was hard to read; he smiled, almost as if what he had to say pleased him. 'Identity fraud picked up way too late. We could do something if we got hold of him, but he keeps a very low profile.'

'Houli said he was under pressure and I believed him. I'm wondering who's the greater threat in all this—the Wongs or Houli and his mate?'

'Interchangeable,' Chang said.

Ali shook his head. 'I've lost count of the number of people Houli has terrified.'

'About what?' I said.

'Money, what else? Not having it, losing it, owing it. The immigrant's greatest vulnerability.'

'Hardy,' Chang said, 'we're not going to get any-where unless you tell us who contacted you in the first place. That's where this particular skein starts—we've got a mysterious disappearance that may mask a murder, a definite murder, that's Nordlung, and a serious assault on you. Who was it?'

I thought hard about it while they waited. I had no contract with Standish and no real obligation. No money had changed hands and, after what his wife had said, there was reason to think he didn't have the money to pay me anyway. I had no professional reputation to safeguard, but somehow all that didn't count for much. The habit of protecting the person who'd assigned a job to me was ingrained. As well, I remembered the way Standish had looked in the restaurant. Evidently Chang still hadn't checked with Caulfield.

I shook my head. 'I'm sorry, Stephen. I can't tell you. Not yet anyway. Give me some time to check on a few things. Maybe then.'

Chang looked at Ali. 'Told you.'

'Tell you one thing, I think the place they took me was underneath the Tiberias Club. I recognised the music.'

'Big deal,' Ali said. 'How about holding him on the drugs charges until he cooperates?'

Chang said, 'No, I blew any chance of that when I arranged for him to be brought here. We'll just have to wait until he fucks up again and hope that tells us something useful.'

'They tell me I could've died if I'd been dumped in a lockup overnight. Thanks.'

But they were already on their way out. Chang turned at the door. 'I'm beginning to wish I'd left you there.'

11

I was in hospital for over a week. I didn't have a ruptured spleen, and the doctor told me my broken eardrum wasn't infected and would repair itself in time. He confirmed what I'd said; I appeared to be a good healer. I'm the least metaphysical person I know, but I tend to believe that recovering from injury or illness is partly a state of mind thing. I wanted badly to heal.

Frank Parker and my lawyer Viv Garner visited—still no grapes. I walked the corridors. Megan brought in books, pyjamas and my medications. I abandoned the Miles Franklin winner and read a biography of Bernard Spilsbury, the famous English pathologist, and re-read George Shipway's *Knight in Anarchy*, one of the best historical novels ever.

Early in the morning, Megan brought in some clothes, my wallet and cheque book, and I got out of the hospital with a credit bank balance, just. Doctor Rasamussen, still looking weary, told me to take it easy and to watch my blood pressure.

'Don't get excited,' he said.

'What if I get a hole in one?'

'That'd be an exception.'

'It sure would.' I didn't tell him that I didn't play golf.

We went to the car park and I found that Megan had driven my 1988 Falcon. She settled herself behind the steering wheel.

'I've been driving it around a bit to keep it running. I love this car. Are you going to leave it to me in your will?'

'No, I'll leave it to the kid.'

She patted her belly. 'Fair enough. I won't say a word about what you do next, but don't even think about putting Hank in any danger. I'm not interested in being a single mother.'

I settled in at home, threw out some old food and made a list of new stuff to buy. I went to the gym for a very light session and Wesley swore when he saw my injuries.

'You're getting too old for this shit, man.'

I stepped on the scales. 'You're right. Hey, I've lost some weight.'

'Could be in your brain.'

* * *

I'd asked Megan to bring in my mobile but she'd said she couldn't find it even though she'd rung it and listened for the signal. Not surprising; I often couldn't find it myself. I hate the thing. But I hunted around and eventually found it under a couple of CDs that had slid over it on the desk where I'd left it turned off after downloading the photographs of Houli. I thumbed it on and the blinking symbol told me there were unanswered calls.

'Hardy! This is Miles Standish. Please call me.'

'Hardy. Standish. Where the hell are you?'

There were two others like that, getting more agitated. I punched in his number.

'Yes?'

'Standish, this is Hardy, what—?'

'Jesus Christ! I've been ringing—'

I cut him off. 'I've been in hospital after being bloody nearly killed by that Lebanese bastard you know so well. Don't come on strong with me, mate. You went into smoke. Are you still holed up in McMahons Point with your girlfriend?'

'How the hell did you know that?'

'Never mind. You drop out of sight and now it's all about where I am. What's the trouble?'

'My life's in danger.'

'Our lives are in danger all the time.'

'This is no joke. I need your help.'

The original 'me' guy—absolutely no interest in others. 'I'm not sure I can help you or if I want to. You didn't exactly tell me much of the truth at our first meeting.'

'I suppose not, but I thought we had an arrangement.'

'Yeah, perhaps we do. But I'll want to know all about your dealings with Nordlung—you and May Ling and Freddy Wong and Selim Houli—before you tell me your problem. By the way, your wife thinks you killed Richard Malouf.'

'She's crazy. But Jesus, how do you know—?'

'I was doing my job. I'll meet you at your office.'

'No!'

'Where, then?'

He named an apartment block at Darling Harbour. I knew it as a place publishers and movie people used to accommodate their big-name visitors to Sydney. I'd done some bodyguarding for a couple of these types. Standish gave me the number of his apartment. He was calmer but still edgy. I didn't want him calm.

'Will May Ling be there?'

'I . . . I don't know.'

'Have you got any money?'

'I can get some. How much?'

'As much as you can rustle up. I'll be there in an hour.'

I wanted Standish to be as rattled and vulnerable as possible if I was to find out what was going on. Frightened was good, too, and he was clearly that already. And I thought it wouldn't do any harm to have money in my pocket because I had a need for some right then.

Along with my PEA licence went my right to carry a gun. I'd had an illicit one for a while until, after a nasty confrontation two years earlier, I'd thrown it into Balmoral Bay. But I didn't fancy going off to visit Standish, who had dealings with the Wongs and Houli, unarmed, so for the second time I broke a serious law and bought a .22 Ruger Bearcat pistol from an ex-biker named Ben Corbett.

Corbett, a paraplegic following an accident, lived in a below-ground flat in Erskineville. He didn't want to let me have the gun without payment up front, but I persuaded him with a bottle of Bundy and a packet of Drum.

'I'm only renting it, Ben,' I said. 'You'll get it back with five hundred—'

'Six hundred.'

'OK, six. In a couple of days—unfired, I hope.'

'You're a wanker, Hardy. What happened to your fuckin' ear?'

I still had a dressing on the ear that Yusef had battered and torn. 'A dog bit it.'

Corbett snuffed out his rollie and took a big slurp of his rum and Coke. 'You're a wanker, Hardy.'

He never had much of a way with words.

The Meridian Apartments were reached via a bridge across the lower reaches of the city streets to Darling Harbour.

With money coming in, I got as close as I could by taxi because parking was impossible. I walked across the bridge in the cool blustery wind wearing an old bomber jacket with the .22 deep in the torn lining of one of the interior pockets. I still had aches and pains, but who hasn't in their mature years? Rain threatened and the water was a dingy grey. I had no real reason to feel encouraged, but I was keen to meet Standish. I had a lot of questions, and forcing my way to answers was what I did best.

Standish opened the door to my knock and I was shocked at his appearance. Gone were the boyish bounce and the confident manner. His tan had a yellow tinge and his shoulders drooped, reducing his height. He was in shirt-sleeves and the shirt wasn't fresh. His pants were wrinkled and his shoes were scuffed. No tie. Some don't look right with a tie and some look wrong without one—Standish was one of these. I'd been prepared to bully him but there was no need.

In size and décor, the apartment was more suited to a writer than an actor or rock star, and Standish had made it look more middle range than it really was by his sloppiness. Clothes, newspapers and magazines were scattered around the living room and there were glasses, coffee cups and takeaway food containers he hadn't bothered to bin or put away in the kitchenette.

I didn't have to ask whether May Ling was there—she wouldn't have been able to tolerate a pigsty like this for a minute. Standish slumped into a chair and waved me to another. I walked to the window and looked out over the water.

With my back to him I said, 'Who do you think wants to kill you?'

'Freddy Wong and Selim Houli.'

'Unless?'

'Why d'you say that?'

'Either of them could do it with no trouble at all, so there must be an unless or an if not about it.'

'You're right. Unless I can find Richard Malouf for them.'

Square one, I thought. 'Why do they want him?'

'I don't know.'

'You must have some idea.'

'I don't. I thought that they might be other victims of his swindle but they said not. May Ling is Freddy Wong's cousin. When she heard that I'd hired you to find Malouf she told Freddy. She tells him everything—he's got some kind of hold over her. I just wanted you to follow up on Stefan's story about seeing Malouf but then the shit hit the fan. Stefan got killed. May Ling said we were both in danger. I had to meet with Freddy Wong or she'd . . . something horrible'd happen to her. Then Houli turned up and the threats came thick and fast. It was only May who stopped them from . . . What happened to you?'

It was as if he'd just remembered I'd told him I'd been injured. I gave him some of the details and he looked more frightened than ever.

His voice, previously a powerful instrument of charm and persuasion, shook. 'I had to pretend I had other ways to find Malouf but I don't. I don't!'

'Take it easy,' I said. 'Got anything to drink here?'

'Scotch, in the kitchen.'

I found a couple of clean glasses and a bottle of Dewar's. Ice cubes in the fridge. I prepared two solid drinks and brought them back to where Standish was sitting with his head bowed low. His wife had said how much he loved to win and hated to lose and he was acting the part now for all he was worth.

'Have a drink,' I said. 'Find Malouf and we're home free.'

He gulped at the drink and almost choked. 'How can you say that? What if he's dead?'

'Do you think he's dead?'

'I hope so. If you . . . we . . . can prove that then those vicious bastards should leave me alone.'

It was interesting to watch him coming out of his state of fear. As soon as he saw a possibility of personal safety his spirits rose. May Ling, I noticed, had dropped out of the equation; I had never been in it.

It was warm in the room and I slipped out of my jacket and reached to hang it over the back of the chair. It fell with a thud. Standish had finished his drink and was on the way to the kitchen for a refill. He picked up the jacket and the pistol dropped into his hand. He stared at it, looking more frightened than ever.

'You think you need this?'

I took it and put it back in the jacket. 'It's just for show. What you need to do is pull yourself together. Go back to work and your own place. If Wong or Houli gets in touch, play for time.'

'I thought you might . . . what will you be doing?'

'What you hired me for originally—trying to find Malouf. You said you'd get some money.'

He gave me a thousand dollars in hundreds. Strange to say it seemed to make him happier.

12

I scouted the area, no sign of anyone watching the apartments. There's a rule in investigation that holds true about half the time—like most rules: test the weakest link. As things stood that was Rosemary Malouf. She'd gone to water after a question or two and had summoned support. The more I thought about it the more it seemed as if this was the place to probe.

Houli was one of those who'd given weight to the theory that Richard Malouf had serious problems by claiming he'd won a lot of money from him. Rosemary Malouf had identified the body. What was the connection between those facts? It was hard to see them as collaborators. From what I'd experienced at Houli's hands it was more likely he'd intimidated her, was controlling her in some way.

A ride in a near-empty bus is good for contemplation and speculation. Suppose Malouf was alive and his apparent death had been contrived somehow. By whom? Houli or Wong, or both? Why, and how it went wrong, allowing that this supposition was correct, were the questions.

I looked through my notes and clippings again and rang Prospero Sabatini.

'Hardy, about time I heard from you. What's been going on?'

'Quite a few things, which I could tell you off the record. Nothing at all on the record.'

'Bloody hell. All right. At least you got in touch. Fill me in.'

I told him as much as I thought I should, still not mentioning Standish, but bringing Freddy Wong and Selim Houli into the picture as well as Chang and Ali.

'You might talk to Chang without telling him who put you on to him,' I said. 'You might get something interesting.'

'Might, might, might. Might doesn't write stories. You say you're still thinking Malouf could be alive. That's the crux. Anything solid there?'

'Not really, and that's where I need your help.'

'You haven't built up much credit.'

'Yes or no?'

'Go ahead, ask.'

I reminded him that in one of his articles he'd mentioned that Malouf's wife had left their home in Gladesville.

'That's right, she couldn't handle the media pressure. The time I talked to her I told her it wouldn't last much longer but she didn't listen.'

'Do you know where she went? That's what I'm asking.'

There was a silence at the end of the line and I could imagine what he was thinking. *What's he up to and what's in it for me?* When it came, his response surprised me.

'She's very vulnerable, Hardy.'

I almost said I knew, but remembered that I'd edited my meeting with her out of my story. 'She's had time to get over it,' I said, 'and I can be gentle when necessary.'

'I bet.'

'Look, she's either on the edge or in the middle of something very nasty. Maybe she knows nothing about it at all. If that's right I'll talk to her and say goodbye. If she's in danger I'll bring the cops in. That's a promise.'

'I can't help you.' He hung up.

I was losing my touch and running out of allies. I'd put the phone too close to my damaged ear and it was hurting. Sitting too long in one position stiffened me, and all the places where Yusef had hit me ached. I was angry. Time to play dirty. I called the Bondi Junction travel agency. Troy answered.

'Mrs Malouf, please.'

'Can I say who's calling?'

I got as close to Perry's soft voice as I could. 'Perry Hassan. Her late husband worked for me.'

She came on the line. 'Yes, Mr Hassan?'

'Sorry to trouble you, Mrs Malouf, but there are some papers I need you to sign. There's some money coming your way.'

'How? I don't understand.'

'I'll explain, but it's urgent. This needs to be handled today to cope with the time difference between here and the UK. I'm tied up now, but I could bring them to you after office hours if you give me your address.'

I was guessing money would be a problem for her. I couldn't see Malouf leaving her with a nest egg. After a very brief hesitation she gave me an address. I thanked her and said I'd see her around seven pm. I wasn't proud of myself when I put down the phone, but my ear and mid-section still hurt and she was the one who'd sicced Yusef on to me.

The address was in Dulwich Hill, a little cul-de-sac off Livingstone Road. I scouted it: a single-fronted cottage with a neat garden at the front and a laneway behind. Some of the houses had driveways and there were few cars in the street. Good lighting. I parked in a nearby street and let the minutes tick by. I was on the doorstep at seven pm precisely and rang the bell. Footsteps.

'Who is it?'

'Perry Hassan.'

The door opened and I pushed it in and bustled the little woman away. She squealed and I kicked the door closed. She raced down the hall, flung open a door, and snatched up her mobile from a table. I clamped her wrist and took it from her.

'I'm not going to hurt you,' I said.

'You *are* hurting me.'

I released her and pointed to my ear while lifting my windcheater up to show the yellow and blue bruise across my middle.

'My eardrum's broken and the ear is only held on by stitches. This is where they hit me—those people you sent after me. You owe me some explanation.'

She was still in her business clothes, minus the jacket and the heels. In slippers, she didn't come up to my shoulder. She slumped down into a chair and covered her face with her hands. I pulled the hands away roughly.

'Don't do that. You're in trouble, Mrs Malouf. Maybe I can help you, but first you have to tell me about your dealings with Selim Houli.'

She looked up at me, big grey eyes pleading in a small, terrified face. 'I can't. They'll kill me.'

'I can arrange protection for you. I told you I'm working with the police.'

She snorted and scrabbled in her bag on the table for a packet of cigarettes. She lit up and blew smoke through her nostrils. 'The police,' she said, 'they aren't worried about the police. They've got . . .'

'What?'

'Their people inside the police.'

I said, 'That might be true, but there are honest police.'

She smiled and blew more smoke. She was gaining confidence. 'And you know them, do you?'

I hesitated just a beat too long.

'I thought so,' she said. 'How can you know? I'll tell you something, Mr . . . who are you again?'

'My name's Hardy.'

'Mr Hardy, I've learned something this year. You can't trust anyone. I was married to a man I thought I knew and I found out that I didn't know him at all. I didn't even know his real name. How's that for trust?'

I pulled out a chair and sat. I slid the ashtray closer to her. My windcheater was still rucked up and I pulled it down. At least she was talking.

'Tell me about it,' I said. 'I do have experience at helping people in tight corners. I do have influential friends I can trust.'

She studied me as she took a few drags on her cigarette. She butted it out and lit another one. 'There's a bottle of wine in the fridge. I need a drink. Would you mind? Don't worry, I'm not going to scoot off.'

I went through to the kitchen, found the chardonnay and a couple of glasses and brought them back to where she was sitting. I poured and sat.

'I married . . . Richard five years ago. I was a flight attendant with Qantas and I met him on a flight back from Dubai. It happens. He was working in the finance industry and seemed to have plenty of money and lots of time. I kept working for almost a year while we carried on the affair but it wasn't satisfactory, as you can imagine.

So we got married and I took a job in a travel agency.

'After another year or so Richard had an affair with the wife of his boss and he got the sack. I forgave him. I loved him. Then he went to work for Perry Hassan. It was a good job in terms of status and money and he seemed happy in it for a time. He worked very hard—incredible hours. He started to drink and gamble. We argued a lot, almost broke up, got back together. He was sexually . . . compelling.'

The third person to say something similar and the second woman.

'Breaking up and getting back together can add spice,' I said. 'I've been there.'

'Mmm, but it was more than just that. You'd have to have seen him in action to understand.'

In fact I had. I remembered the way several women in Perry's office had looked at Malouf as he moved around. Looked quickly and then away. He had a word for a couple of them as we went out for a cup of coffee and they smiled as if he'd given them a bunch of flowers. At the coffee shop he got immediate service from a waitress who stood as close to him as she could. The thing was, as I'd said to Standish, he wasn't extraordinarily handsome and there wasn't any conceit to him. He seemed not to notice the effect he had on women; he certainly didn't play to it, and that attitude appeared to have a powerful effect on them.

'You noticed, didn't you?' she said.

I nodded.

'Shit. It wasn't his looks or his voice, that was just foreplay. His touch was . . . electric. I'm sorry.'

She finished her cigarette and drank some wine. She was naturally pale, but the wine brought a little colour into her face. As she forced herself to relax, I saw how attractive she could be under the right conditions. Her hair was a rich auburn and thick and her features were generous when not under strain. The wine was OK; I poured some more for both of us.

'After a while, it was a marriage in name only. I left a couple of times but he always managed to draw me back. He said he needed me, but he always needed plenty of others. I thought I was pregnant at one point and that brought me back. I wasn't and that just about finished us off.'

She paused and I nodded, letting her tell it at her own pace.

'He was under a lot of stress; he worked all night at the computer sometimes and wouldn't tell me what he was doing. I heard him on the phone a few times speaking Lebanese and Chinese. Then I wouldn't see him for days.'

'Chinese?'

She shrugged. 'Yes, you pick up a few words as flight crew. I wanted to ask him about it but by then I was . . . afraid of him. God, I'm spilling my guts, aren't I? How've you managed to get me talking like this?'

'I'm a good listener.'

She smiled for the first time. 'I hope you're a bit more

than that. You'll need to be. Anyway, I hadn't seen him for almost a week and then Selim Houli and another man paid me a visit at home. Houli asked me if I knew where Richard was and I said I didn't. They searched Richard's office and spent a long time at his computer. Then Houli said Richard was in a lot of trouble and that Richard Malouf was not his real name. He gave me a mobile number and said if Richard . . . if he contacted me I was to call him immediately—immediately.'

I could imagine the threat that accompanied the demand and the memory of it brought a nervous twitch to her hands.

'I asked why would I do that and he said that if I didn't he'd have acid thrown in my face. He showed me photographs of people who'd suffered that and how the surveillance of them had been done. He said the same thing would happen if I spoke to the police. I'm not a brave person and I believed him.'

I nodded. 'I can see why you would. What happened then?'

'Houli came again and told me the police would be arriving soon to ask me to identify a body they believed to be Richard. Houli told me to make the identification or the same threat would be carried out. I did what he said.'

We'd worked our way through two-thirds of the wine but she hadn't smoked since she began talking. Now she lit one. Her hands were steady and she blew a strong stream of smoke well away from me.

'I gave up smoking when I met him. He didn't like it.' She laughed. 'He wasn't who he said he was; he rooted around; he embezzled millions of dollars; he was involved with gangsters and I let him tell me what to do. How dumb can you get?'

'You know what I have to ask you next.'

'Before you do, what's your interest in all this? Did he steal your money?'

'Yes, but it's more complicated than that. There's something big going on. Then there's what Houli did to me.'

'I'm sorry about that. All right, you want to know whether that was the man I knew as Richard Malouf in the morgue?'

'Yes.'

'It wasn't.'

13

She said Houli had made the same threat—acid in the face—to compel her to contact him if anyone came asking about Richard Malouf after the initial fuss had died down.

'That's what I did when you turned up.'

'I understand. Does Houli know that you've moved here?'

'I don't know. I had to rent out the Gladesville house because I couldn't afford the mortgage. Richard had handled that and I had no idea it was so high. You found me easily enough, so I suppose Houli could. He could follow me from work, for example.'

She put her hand to her face and I knew what she was thinking about.

'I suppose talking to you'd come under the same heading as talking to the police or not telling him about anyone enquiring after Richard. I don't know why I'm doing it.'

I did. Even people under as serious a threat as she was can bottle things up for only so long. Eventually the pressure has to be relieved, but it would have sounded patronising to tell her so.

'Before we get on to how to protect you, Mrs Malouf, I've got another question. When you said you didn't know where your husband was, was that true?'

'It was then, but I've had time to think about it.'

'And . . . ?'

Her smile was professional—the kind an airline hostess or a travel agent might use to comfort a passenger or sell a package.

'Let's talk about the protection first.'

I'd been thinking about it and had come up with two ideas. 'Do you remember a journalist named Prospero Sabatini?'

She was about to finish the wine in her glass but she stopped and gave me a quizzical look. 'How the hell did you know about that?'

'I don't know anything, but I spoke to him and—'

'He didn't tell you . . . no, of course not, you tricked me.'

'I tried to get him to help me find you but he wouldn't.'

Her smile now was entirely different. 'That's nice.'

'I was just guessing that you meant something to him. But it's more than that, right?'

She poured out the rest of the wine. Well, it wasn't a full bottle to start with.

'It's weird,' she said. 'I met Pros in a bookshop one night during one of my separations from Richard. We were both after the same book and they only had the one copy. He let me have it. We went for coffee and got along very well. I met him again and gave him the book. I'm pretty sure something could have happened but . . . Richard came back and that was it. He phoned me after . . . the death, but I was too afraid to really talk to him. What're you thinking?'

'That he might help. Might give you a place to stay that Houli doesn't know about.'

I could see the idea appealed to her but she shook her head. 'I still have to get about, go to work, buy bloody food.'

That led to my other idea. I told her about the task force Chang was heading up and its brief to investigate the connection between Chinese and Lebanese crime. I said Chang had resources and manpower. If he was convinced that Malouf was some kind of lynchpin he could provide her with protection.

'Houli and a gangster named Freddy Wong are both trying to find Richard Malouf,' I said. 'And you heard him speaking Chinese and Lebanese. I think Inspector Chang will find that of great interest.'

She thought about it. This time she didn't touch her face or smoke or drink, but from her eyes I could tell that she was weighing a number of things in the balance. Time had dragged on and it was cold in the unheated room. She shivered, but not from the cold.

'You're a bit of a shit for all your winning ways, aren't you? That's the deal, eh? Protection in return for information?'

'Put it that way if you want to, yes. But I'm taking you on trust that you do have something to contribute.'

'You could twist a corkscrew straight. All right, you set everything up the way you said and I'll tell you something.'

It took a series of phone calls—to Sabatini, to Chang, from Chang to others and back to me, but eventually the arrangements were made.

We were both edgy, but on first name terms by then and drinking coffee as she packed a couple of bags. She had the flat on loan from a friend who was overseas, and she hadn't brought a lot of stuff with her. No problem about leaving. She'd had her mail diverted to her business address and didn't have a landline to the flat.

In the hook-up, she'd spoken briefly to Sabatini and was having trouble suppressing her excitement at the prospect of seeing him again. I had to tell Sabatini I couldn't promise any scoops, but he was smart enough to know that he was, to some extent, on the inside now. Anyway, he seemed as enthusiastic as Rosemary about them meeting.

Sabatini lived in Coogee, handy to Rosemary's office. She didn't have a car. She told me that the Merc Richard Malouf had run was repossessed by a finance company after he went missing. I drove her and we had a discreet police escort.

'He told me he owned the Mercedes,' she said as we headed east. 'I'm trying to think of one thing he told me that was true or even partly true.'

'He must have been a good actor,' I said.

'Mmm, whoever he was.'

'You only have Houli's word on that.'

Her laugh was nervous. For all her eagerness to see Sabatini, she was aware that she was on dangerous ground and Houli's name had triggered that fear. 'It's funny,' she said, 'but I'm inclined to believe that bloody gangster rather than the man I was married to. *If* I was married. Shit, what a mess.'

She pulled out her cigarettes and lit up. I wondered what Sabatini's attitude was to smoking. She glanced back at the police car.

'How do you know you can trust these particular police?'

'Instinct,' I said.

'Jesus Christ, I'm not sure about this. What if . . . ?'

'We're here.' I pulled up outside a small block of flats a few streets back from the beach. The police car slid in behind us and two uniformed officers escorted us to the entrance. Sabatini was in flat 4. I rang, he answered, and the security door opened. We took the stairs to the second level and I knocked. Sabatini, in jeans, sneakers and a jumper, appeared. He'd trimmed his beard and smelled of the shower and shampoo.

'Hello, Pros,' Rosemary said.

'Hello, Rose, Hardy. Come in.'

The senior cop said they'd be on watch in the street.

'Thank you,' Rosemary said.

'I'm off,' I said. 'Remember, Rosemary, there's a meeting tomorrow at nine am.'

'Yes,' she said, 'I can't say I'm looking forward to it, but at least I feel I've broken out of some kind of prison.'

Rosemary's words stayed in my head as I drove home. It hadn't occurred to me before, but they amounted to a pretty good description of the condition of a lot of the people I'd dealt with in my work: the parents of missing children, the blackmailed, the threatened. And it applied not only to the innocent—the liars and cheats made prisons for themselves and squirmed to get out of them.

Those thoughts led inevitably to me considering my own position. Was I in a prison of my own or somebody else's making? I wasn't usually given to negative self-examination and I shook the impulse off. I was working, possibly being of help to people, and I had scores to settle. That was enough on the positive side. For the rest of the way home, I played the new Dylan album Megan had left in the CD slot. The voice was just a growl now, but a great growl:

. . . *it's all good.*

14

The next morning Chang, Ali and a technician assembled audio and visual recording gear in Sabatini's living room.

'This is highly unorthodox,' Chang said, 'but so is this whole thing.'

Rosemary and Sabatini smiled at each other. They held coffee cups and were relaxed. It was good to see. I remembered what it was like—that first firing up of a new relationship—but it seemed like a long time ago. The flat was spacious, tastefully decorated with an emphasis on books and CDs. I browsed—fiction and history, biography and economics, blues and soul—my kind of guy apart from the economics. The day was cloudy with rain threatening so the view of the water wasn't inspiring, but it'd still have put thousands on the price or the rent.

'OK,' Chang said. 'I don't think Mr Sabatini should be present. I could do without Mr Hardy, but—'

'I want them both here.'

'You should have a lawyer,' Sabatini said.

'You've been through this sort of thing before, haven't you, Cliff?' Rosemary said.

'A few times.'

'You can warn me of the pitfalls.'

Chang shrugged. We took chairs around the table where the recording devices were set up and Chang made the standard introduction: time, date, place and list of those present. He asked Rosemary to detail her contacts with Selim Houli, giving dates and times as accurately as she could. Rosemary went through it more or less as she'd told me with a few extra details and specific words used. Chang was good; he interrupted her very seldom. Ali asked if she could remember anything of the Lebanese Richard Malouf had used on the phone and Rosemary rattled off a few phrases. Ali nodded. That prompted Chang to ask the same question about Chinese, and Rosemary hesitated before speaking a few words. Chang smiled and he broke the flow again only when he asked for Houli's mobile number.

'It's on my phone,' Rosemary said.

'I'll get it.' Sabatini went into what was obviously one of the bedrooms. Neither Chang, nor Ali nor the technician or I moved a muscle. Sabatini handed Rosemary the phone and she brought up the number and recited it to Chang who thanked her. After she admitted making the false identification she stopped.

'Is that a crime?' she said.

'I'm sure it is,' Chang said. 'But I wouldn't worry about it. Now, Mrs Malouf, you told Mr Hardy there was something you'd forgotten . . . held back from Houli. I need to know what that was.'

Rosemary didn't milk it, or not very much. She put down her coffee cup and spoke directly into the microphone.

'Richard had a boat,' she said.

part two

15

'I hate boats,' Rosemary said. 'Nasty, smelly things that crash into each other and sink.'

Sabatini smiled; he'd have smiled at anything she said.

Chang said, 'The name of the boat?'

'Something to do with sport . . . *High Fives*, that's it!'

'*High Fives* or *High Five*?' the technician said.

'I don't know. I didn't even know it existed until I found a certificate of some kind in his study. It had fallen down behind a slightly warped skirting board, or maybe it was hidden there. I don't know. But it was insured in his name for a lot of money.'

'And you never mentioned this to Houli?' Chang said.

'No. I didn't find the certificate until a while after he did his rampage and I sort of forgot about it. I was so pissed off at Richard, and so frightened that I probably would have told him if I'd thought about it, but I didn't.'

'Where's this certificate now?' Ali asked.

Rosemary looked defiant. 'The boat was insured for three-quarters of a million dollars and I didn't even know he had it. I was so angry I burned the certificate.'

Chang pressed for more and Ali became almost aggressive, but the interview petered out after that. Rosemary went to work with a policewoman as escort and guard for the day. The technician packed up and left and Sabatini got ready to go to work.

'I've got some leave coming,' Sabatini said as we left the building. 'Rosemary's got a lot of frequent flyer points. We're thinking of going away for a while. To the US maybe.'

'That'd be a very good idea,' Chang said. 'I can't keep up this level of protection for very long and Houli's bound to hear that she's talking to us.'

Sabatini looked alarmed. 'How?'

Ali smiled. 'We'll tell him. When were you thinking of going?'

'Jesus,' Sabatini said. 'Sounds as if it should be now.'

'Make it soon,' Chang said. 'And stay in touch with Hardy.'

Ali looked as though he wanted to protest against that but he didn't.

Sabatini headed for a bus stop, leaving Chang, Ali and me standing by our cars.

'That was a bit rough,' I said, 'letting her know you'll leak to Houli.'

Ali shrugged. 'I'm not impressed. That wasn't worth much. With a boat he could be anywhere.'

'Or still floating around in the harbour,' I said. 'How're your relations with the water police?'

The glances they exchanged suggested that such relations were non-existent.

'Try to stay out of trouble, Hardy,' Chang said. 'Take your pills and watch your back.'

'I don't rate any protection?'

Chang had turned away; Ali said something presumably abusive, in a language I didn't understand. Annoyed by some small leaves drifting from a street tree and clinging to his suit, he brushed them off and swore at the mark they left behind. From the look he gave me I was to blame.

16

Boats. I pretty much shared Rosemary Malouf's feelings about them. I quite liked watching the start of the Sydney to Hobart yacht race from somewhere comfortable with a drink in my hand, but that's about as far as my interest went. I'd been invited aboard a small yacht once for a race on the harbour and found it a mixture of utter boredom and frantic activity. Not my scene. Big toys.

Chang and Ali's team had the resources to track down the details of Malouf's boat, although I suspected it would be a painstaking and slow business, and locating it even more so. I had another tack to try—Gretchen Nordlung.

Nordlung was a yachtsman and he was the one who'd allegedly spotted Richard Malouf. Aboard a yacht? At some yachtie hangout? Maybe the widow would know and sufficient time had elapsed to take the hard edge off her grieving. I had the address and phone number but

123

I needed a way to approach her. I Googled Nordlung and found that several obituaries had been published, one in an online yachting magazine. I called it up: the item was accompanied by a photographic spread of people attending Nordlung's funeral.

It's not true that all Asians look alike, or that Anglos can't tell one from another. Over the years I've had dealings with Chinese, Vietnamese and Koreans and the faces of individuals vary as much as with other races. You just have to learn to recognise the features, hair and head shapes in their own right. But one of the magazine photographs, in colour and in sharp focus, was of Gretchen Nordlung. She was slim and elegant in black, and she was the spitting image of May Ling, perhaps even a shade more beautiful.

Standish was back at work, doing whatever it was he did. I phoned and arranged to meet him and May Ling there after office hours. I didn't say why and he didn't ask. Speaking to him reminded me that I hadn't spent any of his money. I took Megan to lunch at Thai Pothong in Newtown. She ordered up a solid meal and tucked into it enthusiastically. No wine, though.

'No morning sickness?' I asked.

'Not a trace, touch wood.'

'What about cravings?'

She waved her fork over her plate. 'Just for food in general. I'm hungry from morning to night. Are you still doing whatever it is you were doing?'

'Yeah, but in a hands-off sort of way. I'm cooperating with the New South Wales Police Service.'

'Bullshit.'

We went for a walk in Camperdown Park. Megan gazed fondly at the infants in strollers and the children playing on the grass. I've never prayed in my life, but if I could I'd have prayed that everything would turn out well for her.

Standish and May Ling were waiting for me in the empty office. Standish seemed to have regained some composure and was nattily dressed again. May Ling wore an olive green pants suit and a strained, almost hostile, expression. Her makeup and hair were perfect and when she moved there was a faint waft of perfume. No one shook hands.

'Drink, Hardy?'

'Sure.'

Standish and I had scotch; May Ling had white wine. We sat around the table in the recess of Standish's office.

'It won't be a surprise to you,' I said, 'that Selim Houli and Freddy Wong have formed some sort of partnership with finding Richard Malouf as a focus.'

They nodded.

'Any further contact from either of them?'

'No,' Standish said.

'I wonder why they've backed off.'

'Who knows? We're just glad they have. What more can you tell us?'

'Malouf's wife made a false identification of the body.'

'Why?' May Ling said.

'Houli terrorised her.'

Standish took a sip of his drink. May Ling watched him. He was pacing himself. 'I can believe that. So Malouf *is* alive.'

'Maybe. At least we know he wasn't the corpse in the car.'

May Ling said, 'Why is he so important?'

'Your cousin Freddy didn't tell you?'

Her sculpted lips tightened. She didn't like me putting it that way but she simply shook her head.

I took a slug of Standish's very good scotch. 'It's the big question. It's what led Freddy and Houli to scare the shit out of you and Houli and his mate to work me over. That's the easy part. Stefan Nordlung was murdered and the man Rosemary Malouf identified was killed as well. It's all connected but we don't know how. The police are working on it.'

Standish almost spilled his drink. 'You didn't . . .'

'Your name hasn't come up so far. I know you've got something to hide, perhaps lots of things. I know you were involved in some dodgy stuff with Nordlung, but unless you actually know where Malouf is—'

'I don't!'

I looked at May Ling. She shook her head, again.

'Are you sure?'

Her fists clenched, the lacquered nails biting into her palms. 'Yes. Yes!'

'Then I don't much care about what you might have been up to. The thing is to find Malouf if it can be done.'

I'd printed out the photograph of Gretchen Nordlung. I put it on the table and leaned back. 'Sister?' I said. 'Another cousin, perhaps?'

The look May Ling gave me would've scaled fish. She put her glass down as if it offended her to be drinking with me. 'I worked for another solicitor before coming to Miles,' she said. 'He had frequent dealings with people in your line of work. Detestable probers into people's lives. Nasty turners-over of rocks.'

'Some rocks need to be disturbed. You haven't answered my question.'

For a moment I thought she was going to turn to Standish for support, but a glance at him showed her that he was interested in her answer too. She came as close to being flustered as I imagine she ever got. The private school accent even slipped a bit. 'Yes, she's my sister. So what?'

'Gretchen.'

'Yes, she's ashamed of being Chinese. I'm surprised she hasn't had her eyes straightened and her hair bleached.'

'I want to talk to her and I want you to pave the way.'

Standish evidently thought it time for him to play a part. 'Why, Hardy?'

'Boats,' I said. 'Boats have a lot to do with all this some-how. I phoned Mrs Nordlung, she told me where her husband was and within an hour he was dead. It looked as though Houli's enforcer Yusef Talat killed him, perhaps scared him to death. Houli's technique seems to be to get people to alert him to what's going on. I want to know if there's a connection between Gretchen Nordlung and Houli, or with Freddy Wong for that matter.'

'I didn't know you had a sister,' Standish said. 'I gather you're not close? You didn't go to Stefan's funeral. He was your brother-in-law.'

May Ling flared, 'Neither did you and he was your client.' She picked up her glass and had another sip. 'I try not to be close, but it's hard in our community to cut yourself off. And she clings, when she needs to, and that can be at any time.'

'Can you arrange to meet her?' I said.

'With you along?'

'Absolutely.'

Standish swilled the dregs of his drink in his glass. He wanted another but he didn't want May Ling to see his need and he didn't want me to see his dependence on her. A tough choice. He reached for the bottle and topped himself up.

'Jesus, Hardy,' he said. 'If . . . Gretchen is under Houli or Freddy's control they're likely to turn up at this meeting.'

I nodded. 'That'd be interesting, wouldn't it?'

May Ling looked worried, a frown line disturbing the satin-smooth brow. 'What game are you playing?'

'The only one I know,' I said. 'Push the buttons and see what pops.'

17

The venue for the meeting, at lunch the following day, was a café at Circular Quay. Fine by me; plenty of people about and I like to see the ferries at work. A bit of didgeridoo goes down well, too. It wasn't quite May Ling's kind of place though, a touch too much of the common people, and she struck me as an indoors woman, the place where she did her best work. That complexion hadn't been subjected much to sun, wind and rain. A bit of a threat on this day. The winter sun was strong and she had mounted massive protection—a broad brimmed hat and sunglasses that seemed to cover most of her face.

She'd dressed down for the occasion in trousers, medium heels and a sweater and I wondered what this meant about her relationship with her sister. The scarf and gloves she wore added a touch of elegance, but she clearly wasn't trying to outshine another woman.

I watched her approach, cleaving through the tourists and lunchtimers, expecting them to part, which they mostly did.

'Mr Hardy,' she said as she deposited her bag on the table and took off her gloves.

'Ms Ling,' I said. 'Sydney at its best.'

'Which puts it way behind a lot of other places.'

'You think so? I don't agree.'

'You wouldn't. I hope you're ready for . . . Gretchen. She devours men.'

'Why here? She lives in Seaforth.'

'So she's a bit out of her comfort zone. Gretchen'll find this very tacky . . .'

'She'll have trouble parking her Beemer or Porsche or whatever.'

'Taxi. She's lost her licence at least twice. She's a maniac driver.'

Unlike you, I thought. 'Devours men, you say—is that why you never told Miles about her?'

She ignored that and glanced around for a waiter. 'I'm betting the service here is sub-standard.'

'I've got a carafe of the house white coming. What was her name before she changed it?'

'I forget. Why don't you ask her if you want to get off on the wrong foot. Here she comes.'

I could see why May Ling hadn't chosen to compete with her sister. There was no chance of winning. The photograph in the magazine hadn't done her any justice. There was no other way to describe her but as exquisitely beautiful. I caught an amused look on May Ling's face as I got to my feet. For her, I'd only made a sketchily polite gesture. This woman could pull the strings.

'Why, May, honey, how nice to see you in such rugged and polite company.'

'Cliff Hardy,' May Ling said, 'this is Gretchen Nordlung. Gretchen spent a little time in San Francisco and she likes to let it show.'

Gretchen smiled at me, showing perfect teeth, perfect eyes, perfect lips. The effect was overwhelming and, strangely, almost comic. 'Bitch,' she said. 'Where's your fancy lawyer, and who's this thug? I'll give you ten minutes.'

Like May Ling, as well as the fragile beauty there was a tough side to her. *Thug might be the only way to play it*, I thought. I remembered the loose, almost sloppy style of her speech on the phone. Nothing like that now. 'I rang you wanting to speak to your husband. You told me where he was. When I got to the marina they were fishing him out of the water.'

'Did you? I've forgotten.'

'I wanted to ask him about his sighting of Richard Malouf. I particularly wanted to know where and when that might have been. Do you know anything about it?'

The carafe of wine arrived and I poured a glass.

'I'm not going to drink that piss,' Gretchen said. 'What's all this about?'

133

'Just answer the question, Sunny,' May Ling said.

Gretchen tensed, her eyes narrowed and suddenly she looked more dangerous than beautiful. 'Don't you call me that!'

'Sorry,' May Ling said. 'I'd forgotten about that chink in your armour.'

The two women glared at each other. A ferry hooted, a waiter hovered nearby, the Aboriginal band tuned up, but they were oblivious to everything except their mutual hostility. I shook my head at the waiter and leaned forward.

'Did your husband tell you he'd seen Richard Malouf?'

'Yes. Yes, but he must have been wrong. Richard's dead.' She picked up the bag she'd put on the floor. 'Is that all?'

'Saw him where?'

'Somewhere on the fucking harbour.'

She'd spoken more loudly than she'd intended, and a couple of heads turned towards us.

'I think your husband was right and Richard Malouf is still alive.'

I don't know what reaction I'd expected but it wasn't the one I got. Her face, a mask of anger and disdain, was suddenly transformed into a picture of confusion and distress. She fumbled in her bag.

'You can't smoke here,' May Ling said.

That left Gretchen reaching for the glass of wine I'd poured. She drank some and spilled some on her dress. 'What . . . what do you mean he's alive?'

It was no time for pussyfooting. 'His wife has admitted that she made a false identification. Under pressure.'

'My God!' Her voice was a whisper; she sat back in her chair and stared out over the quay. She gripped the glass in both hands. A number of rings on her fingers, but no wedding ring.

May Ling struck like a cobra. 'He was your lover, eh, Sunny? Just another one in a long, long line. He came on to me, too. He was slipping it to every willing woman in sight.'

Gretchen didn't respond to her use of the name. In fact, she didn't appear to have heard what her sister said. She drank a little wine, retched, and for a minute it looked as if she'd vomit, but she collected herself. 'I was in love with him,' she said. 'I loved him so much and he promised me we would . . .'

Her head fell forward and she fainted, sliding down in her chair. May Ling was lightning fast and strong. She grabbed Gretchen's arm and supported her before moving to get a better grip. People around, already interested, murmured their concern but May Ling quelled them with a fierce stare.

'She'll be all right,' she said. 'She's a diabetic and the silly bitch doesn't eat enough. Her sugar's always low and a shock can trigger a hypo. Pour some sugar into that wine.'

I poured three sachets of sugar into the half-glass of wine and May Ling forced her sister, coming out of the hypoglycaemic faint, to drink it. A good deal of the liquid spilled on her clothes, but enough went down to bring her around. Her face was damp with sweat and there were wet patches showing under her armpits and spreading. I'd faced the same situation and done the same things for my diabetic mother many times when I was young and was always surprised at how quickly it worked. Gretchen's eyes opened and came back into focus.

'Bloody hypo,' she said. 'That fucking lying wog bastard.'

May Ling nodded. 'Right. Hardy, let's get out of here.'

I put money on the table to pay for the wine. May Ling collected her things and Gretchen's bag and we left the café, supporting her between us. Gretchen was still shaky and didn't protest. The Aboriginal band blasted out its first riffs.

'My car's not far off,' May Ling said. 'I'll take her home.'

'I'm with you all the way,' I said. 'She knows something and I'm not letting her out of my sight.'

We walked to where May Ling's Peugeot was parked and she handed me the keys she'd dug out of her bag.

'You drive. I'll look after her. It's 17 View Street, Seaforth. Use the GPS.'

We bundled Gretchen into the back seat and May Ling slid in beside her. I started the car, switched on the GPS and gave the destination. I familiarised myself with the controls before setting off—nothing makes you feel sillier than activating the wipers when you want to signal a turn.

In one hundred and fifty metres turn . . .

The programmatic female voice soon became irritating, but the directions to an area I knew little about were helpful.

'How's she doing?' I asked.

'She's groggy. Would you believe she hasn't got any glucose with her? Not so much as a bloody jelly bean. How's that for stupid?'

I didn't say anything. My mother had been the same. Denial, but in her case she was sometimes too drunk to remember to carry something with her. She was also capable of injecting too much insulin when under the weather.

I pulled in to a service station along Pitt Road and got a bottle of Coke. May Ling forced Gretchen, against her protests, to sip from it.

'She's coming good,' May Ling said. 'Know about this stuff, do you?'

'One of my many talents.'

May Ling snorted. 'I've been through this so many times, and worse. I don't know about you, but I could do with a drink. There'll be plenty at her place. They were both alcoholics.'

'Unlike someone who needs a drink at one thirty.'

'Fuck you.'

In one hundred and fifty metres, turn . . .

View Street lived up to its name. It afforded a panoramic visual sweep of Middle Harbour from Sugarloaf Bay to Beauty Point, and number 17 was the jewel in the street's crown, if you like that sort of thing. It was built on three levels, all glass and steel and white brick and with a brick driveway flanked by palm trees.

'Hollywood Gothic, isn't it?' said May Ling. She handed me a remote control device that opened the gates. I drove up a steep series of ramps to a garage door twenty metres across.

'Hit it again.'

The door slid open; there were three spaces, one filled with a sporty red Mercedes, one with a trailer carrying a medium-size catamaran and one empty.

'Here we are,' May Ling said, 'where Sun Ling found her pot of gold—a rich man with two quadruple bypasses.'

We got Gretchen into the house, into a living room filled with modernistic furniture. The floor to ceiling windows looked out to the water through slightly tinted glass. May Ling eased her sister into an armchair and left the room. She came back with a small plastic case. She opened it and proceeded to check Gretchen's blood glucose level.

'Coming up,' she said. 'A few brain cells gone maybe but she won't miss them.'

Gretchen glared at her. 'Get me a fucking drink.'

May Ling pointed to the bar. 'Do the honours, Cliff. She'll have gin and just wave the tonic bottle over it. I'll have white wine and you can suit yourself.'

Bombay Sapphire gin, what else? Wolf Blass chardonnay and I took a single malt with a name I couldn't pronounce.

We sat around a glass-topped coffee table on the slightly uncomfortable chairs while the air-conditioning kept the room temperature at perfect and the white carpet showed no signs of dirty footmarks. The big house—a spiral staircase rose from one corner of the room to a mezzanine with two staircases going on up from there—had an eerie feeling of emptiness.

Gretchen knocked back her drink in a couple of swallows and held out her glass. I looked at May Ling.

'Go ahead. It usually takes three or four to put her on her ear.'

I prepared the drink but didn't make it as strong; I wanted her to talk sense. Gretchen took it without thanking me. She looked annoyed at the signs of spillage on her clothes but shrugged. She kicked off her stilettos and tucked her legs up under her. Still limber despite the hypo and the gin.

'Well, this is cosy, sis. The thug's a gun driver and can mix a good drink. How is he in the sack?'

'I wouldn't know,' May Ling said. 'Where we were was that you as good as told us that you were fucking Richard Malouf and that him faking his death, which could be what happened, leaves you feeling angry. What was going on?'

'Why do you care?' Gretchen said.

'I'll tell you why,' I said. 'Two people are dead—your husband, the man who was ID'd as Malouf—and some very heavy people are looking for him. They've terrorised one woman, scared the shit out of May Ling and Miles Standish and put me in hospital. Malouf stole a lot of money from me and other people. I'd like to get it back, but there's other people who're a lot keener.'

Gretchen giggled. The gin was getting to her and I wished I hadn't made the first one so strong, but maybe it was the low sugar having an effect. 'I like the bit about May and Miles being scared shitless.'

May Ling sipped her wine. 'You won't like it so much when I tell Freddy Wong that you were fucking the guy he's looking for so hard.'

Gretchen's face lost colour and I thought she was going to go into another faint. She drained her glass and dropped it onto the floor before wrapping her arms around herself and shaking uncontrollably. May Ling jumped up and went to her.

'Sunny, Sunny, what is it?'

Gretchen half rose from her chair and collapsed into her sister's arms. They clung to each other with Gretchen sobbing softly and May Ling making soothing noises. I felt shut out, invisible. Eventually Gretchen became quiet, passive, and May Ling stayed crouched by her chair. Gretchen drew in a long, painful breath.

'Could you get me a cigarette, May?'

May Ling got the packet from Gretchen's bag, lit a cigarette and handed it to her. Gretchen puffed and then handed it back. May Ling snuffed it out in a big ceramic ashtray on the coffee table.

Gretchen was wearing a blue silk dress with long, loose sleeves buttoned at the wrist. It was still damp with the sweat induced by the hypo. With some difficulty, she undid the button on the left and pushed the sleeve up. Livid injection marks stood out against her smooth, ivory skin.

'Freddy got me hooked,' she said. 'Really hooked. No one else can supply me—no one ever!'

18

May Ling got Gretchen steadied down and onto coffee rather than gin. She worked her way through a good many cigarettes as she told us that Freddy Wong had introduced her to heroin after she'd learned of Malouf's death. She'd been intensely involved with him for some time and she took the news hard. The death of her husband was a second, but minor, shock. When May Ling asked her how she'd become so involved with Freddy, Gretchen had recovered enough to read some signs.

'Freddy's got to you, too, hasn't he? I can tell from the way you reacted to his name. So, you first.'

'Debt. He lent me money,' May Ling said. 'You?'

'Gambling.'

Gretchen said she knew Freddy was dangerous and had always avoided him, but when she took up with Malouf and was drawn into high stakes gambling, she'd caught the bug and got deep in debt to Freddy.

'I've got an addictive personality,' Gretchen said. 'And other problems.'

May Ling bit back a response although her sympathy for her sister was ebbing fast. They were both smoking now, and a fug was building up in the room, something you don't experience much these days. Gretchen lit another cigarette from the butt of her previous one and looked at me.

'Freddy warned me to get in touch with him if anyone made any sort of enquiry about Richard. When you rang, that's what I did. I've wondered ever since whether Freddy killed Stefan and if I'm responsible.'

So Freddy Wong had the same thing going as Houli—an early warning system for when Malouf's name came up. And when the need arose one alerted the other. I was pretty sure Talat had killed Nordlung and presumably after he'd been told everything about the sighting of Malouf.

'That's all your husband told you, was it?' I said. 'That he'd seen Malouf somewhere on the harbour.'

Gretchen nodded. 'It could've been around the harbour somewhere. Stefan liked to drink in various places.'

'What places?' May Ling asked.

Gretchen almost laughed. 'Don't ask me. I hate boats and everything to do with them.'

'So you never went on Malouf's boat?'

That brought another slight smile. 'I didn't say that. His boat was beautifully fitted out . . .'

May Ling said, 'Somewhere to fuck.'

'You should try it.'

I said, 'When you say fitted out, what d'you mean? Apart from the bed?'

'Oh, it had everything—computers, satellite dishes, GPS, television. He had a bunch of mobile phones and he used Skype. He talked fluently to people all over the world.'

'What d'you mean?' I said.

'Well, I heard him speaking Chinese and what sounded like Arabic and Indonesian. I know a bit of Indonesian from going to Bali.'

'What kind of a boat was it? Was it ocean-going?'

Gretchen shrugged. 'I don't know. It was white.'

'Great help,' May Ling said. 'So he had a floating office. Why?'

My thought was different. 'Where did you meet up with him and get on the boat?'

'Different places, different marinas, all around the harbour.'

'At the Spit?'

She gave a lopsided grin, almost a grimace. 'Yes, only when Stefan was away. May, I'm going to need . . .'

'Jesus,' May Ling said, 'you have to get off that stuff, Sunny.'

Gretchen hugged herself and shivered, the classic junkie-in-need pose. 'I don't think I . . .'

'I know a good detox place,' I said.

May Ling nodded. There was a long silence as Gretchen looked at me and back at May Ling, whose face was set implacably. It was obviously a scene she'd played in before.

'Oh yes,' Gretchen whispered. 'But I just need a small hit now.'

'No way,' May Ling said.

We got Gretchen to a clinic in Marrickville I'd had dealings with in the past. My doctor, Ian Sangster, signed the admission form and May Ling acted as guarantor for the fees, next of kin and contact. Gretchen was passive, resigned.

'She's in for a rough time,' I said as we left the clinic. 'Coming off one dependency's bad enough, but three or four . . .'

'Five,' May Ling said. 'She's a sex addict as well. So where did that get us, Cliff?'

'When did I become Cliff?'

'Today. You handled all that very well. My confidence in you has grown.'

'That's nice and I guess you've shown your softer side with your sister, but I'm not sure we're playing on the same team. You want to find Malouf so as to get Houli and Freddy off your back. You don't care what they were up to with Malouf or who killed Stefan Nordlung and the mystery man. Right?'

We were walking along Marrickville Road towards where

I'd parked the Peugeot in a side street. May Ling stopped, slumped into a chair outside a café.

'I'm tired and hungry.'

I was, too. We ordered coffee and sandwiches and we drank and ate steadily without speaking. She finished first, wiped her hands and sniffed at her fingers.

'I haven't smoked for years. Bugger Sunny. I've hauled her out of trouble since she was thirteen and had her first abortion, but she is my sister and I do care about her.'

I nodded. 'Parents?'

'Both dead from overwork. They built up a restaurant and import business from nothing. When they died Freddy managed to take it over—I never found out how. That's why I studied law, to see if I could get it back, but I got sidetracked and Freddy grew too big and nasty to go up against.'

'I can believe that,' I said. 'But you stayed in touch with him, borrowed money.'

'Yes. But getting Sunny hooked, that's just too much. I'll do whatever I can to screw him. So I do want to know why people got killed and why Freddy and Houli are so worked up about Malouf. It's almost as if they're afraid of anyone catching up with him before they do, don't you think? As if they're scared. What was he doing? He obviously wasn't just a smartarse screen jockey who ripped off people like you, too lazy to look after their own investments.'

I laughed. She was clear-headed and unrelenting. That was the moment I decided to trust May Ling sufficiently to share some information with her and Standish and try jointly to get below the surface into what was really going on.

When I got home I phoned Sabatini at his paper and was told he'd gone on leave. I called the Bondi Junction travel agency and spoke to Troy. He told me Rosemary had gone on leave.

'Anyone else asking for her?'

'How do you mean?'

'You remember the man of Middle Eastern appearance who came in a few days ago? Snappy dresser?'

'Yes.'

'Has he asked about her?'

He hung up. My guess the answer was yes, and that Houli or Talat had frightened him. I phoned Standish and told him Houli was likely to be applying pressure and so was Freddy Wong.

'Why?'

'We've taken two women they were dealing with out of circulation. Safely.'

'Who's *we*?'

'Me and the police, me and May Ling. Is she there?'

'No. I don't understand any of this, Hardy. It sounds as if you've just made things worse.'

'Before they get better, let's hope. Have you still got that place at Darling Harbour?'

'Yes, I took it for a month.'

'I suggest you get hold of May Ling and meet me there tonight. We need to have a sort of conference to try to figure out what's going on and what to do. There's more information, but it's hard to interpret. Three heads needed.'

'God, you're a bastard. First you tell me to get back to work and now you want me back in hiding. And what's all this about you and May Ling?'

'Tonight,' I said. 'About eight.'

I phoned Chang and asked if he'd had any luck tracking down Malouf's boat.

'There's no such vessel registered in New South Wales,' he said. 'We're widening the search but I'm not optimistic. I think your informant, to put it politely, was full of shit. I tried to contact her but what d'you know? She and the journo have skipped out and I haven't heard a word about it from you. Not happy, Hardy.'

I couldn't blame him and tossed up whether to add Gretchen Nordlung's confirmation that the boat existed, sketchy though the evidence was. What was the point? May Ling wasn't going to allow him to interview her sister in the clinic and he wasn't likely to take much notice of junkie evidence anyway. I needed more solid information on what Malouf was doing before I could make use of the police again. Chang hung up on me—two in a row.

I chanced my luck and rang Perry Hassan. I asked him if Malouf had dealt with overseas clients and institutions while in his employ. Perry let out an exasperated sigh. 'Not on my behalf,' he said, 'but from what the auditors have turned up he did.'

'Why did you let him?'

'You can't control them. Smart operators like him can play any game they please.'

'Did he handle the business of Lebanese and Chinese clients in Sydney?'

'Of course.'

'D'you know who he dealt with offshore?'

'No, and I don't want to know. Give it a rest, Cliff. I'm struggling to keep my head above water here. Give it a rest.'

At least he didn't hang up.

The apartment had been cleaned and tidied since the last time I was there and Standish himself was looking in better shape. Not quite his old self, but getting there. May Ling had changed her casual outfit for a blouse and a long, dark skirt that set off her slim figure. There was a smell of Asian takeaway in the air and they were drinking coffee laced with French cognac. Standish offered me the same and I accepted.

'May Ling says you were pretty useful today, Hardy,' Standish said. 'Thank you, but I'm still in the dark about your plans now.'

'I don't have any plans. I just want to lay things out to see if we can make any sense of it. Maybe make some guesses?'

May Ling raised an eyebrow. 'Guesses?'

'Some of the best moves have been made on the basis of guesses.'

'And some of the worst,' she said.

'True.'

Standish was impatient. 'This is going nowhere. We know that Houli and Wong are in cahoots. We know that Malouf had dealings with both . . .'

'And with other members of both communities,' May Ling said. 'Finance matters, I suppose; trying to make use of them in their bloody criminal activities—drugs, girls . . .'

Standish nodded and ran with it. 'Getting them into financial difficulties with loans or investments that went sour and then putting pressure on them. But to do what?'

I said, 'To do something that was worth killing two people for and makes it essential to find Malouf.'

We drank our coffee and thought. May Ling shrugged and got up to brew another pot. I wandered over to the window and looked down onto Darling Harbour where boats, moving and stationary, showed lights. There was a famous replica there, I seemed to recall. Captain Cook's *Endeavour* or the *Bounty*? Couldn't remember.

'Is the replica of the *Endeavour* or the *Bounty* down there?' I asked when May Ling had poured the coffee and we'd added cognac.

'Who the hell cares?' Standish said.

May Ling looked at me. 'Why did you ask that?'

'I was thinking about the *Bounty* and the mutiny. It looks as if Malouf mutinied, broke away from Houli and Wong, and set off on his own like Fletcher Christian. It's a new thought—maybe Malouf faked his death to fool Houli and Wong but they had their suspicions.'

'So they're responsible for only one death and not two,' Standish said. 'How does that help us?'

Not much, I thought, but it clarified something at least. May Ling was staring at me as if she could read my mind. It was an uncomfortable feeling but I made use of it.

'May Ling, you know him and what he's capable of. What would it take for you to go hard up against him?'

She shook her head. 'Something big. Something very big.'

'Satellite dishes, Skype, multiple mobiles,' I said. 'Something international.'

Standish groaned. 'Like I said, he could be anywhere.'

I shook my head. 'I don't think so. I think he's in the wind.'

May Ling looked tired all of a sudden. She leaned back in her chair.

'What does that mean?'

'It's an American expression I picked up from novels. It means hiding, but around.'

'Novels,' Standish said.

19

Life is full of surprises and I got one the next morning in the form of a phone call from Felicity Standish.

'Mr Hardy,' she said, 'I think we have unfinished business.'

I'd heard that before—mostly from people who wanted to do me harm. Did Felicity want to do me harm? I was dealing with a mouthful of water trying to wash down one of my pills stuck in my throat and wasn't my most gracious.

'How's that?' I grunted.

'Well, Miles has been in touch. In fact he's been rather nice to me and the children. I'm wondering whether dealing with you has had a good effect on him.'

My throat wouldn't clear and I barked something, away from the phone.

'What was that?' she said, alarmed.

'It's all right, Mrs Standish, I . . .'

'I use my maiden name, Pargetter, now.'

'Ms Pargetter, I've been in touch with your husband. But thank you for the information. Is there anything else?'

'Yes. I think you're right about Richard Malouf and I believe I can help you find him.'

That was a lot to accept in one bite and my response must have sounded sceptical.

'You don't believe me,' she said.

'I want to, but a lot's happened since we last spoke.'

'I should hope so. You were at square one back then.'

'Can you give me some idea . . .'

'No. I want to meet with you and lay down some ground rules. I've arranged for the children to be collected by Miles's mother. I've got a free day. Will I come to you or do you want to come here?'

She was holding the cards but I didn't want to let her run the whole game. I told her that I'd prefer her to come to me and she agreed. I gave her the address.

'Good old Glebe,' she said. 'I had some good times there in my uni days. I'll be an hour or a bit less.'

It took her forty minutes. She bustled in, all designer jeans, high-heeled boots, red shirt and bomber jacket.

'This is amazing,' she said.

'What is?'

'We used to rent a house in this street when we were

students. A bit further down, towards the water. I didn't know we had a famous private detective for a neighbour.'

'I keep a low profile, Mrs . . . Ms Pargetter. Coffee?'

'Felicity, and yes, please.'

'It won't be up to your standard.'

'I don't care about standards, not anymore.'

I pondered that as I made the coffee. There was something almost hectic about her, as if she was racing ahead and trying to catch up with herself. I brought the coffee into the sitting room, cleared the usual mess of papers and books and we sat opposite each other. She added milk to her coffee, sipped and didn't make a face. Control. I make bitter coffee, can't help it.

'I no longer think Miles killed Richard Malouf,' she said.

'Why not?'

'I've talked to him. He's told me something of what you've been doing on his behalf and . . . other things. I'm convinced. I was jealous and irrational when I said that.'

'And you're not jealous now?'

She smiled. 'That's a sly question. Oh, it's warm in here.'

The room warms up, even in winter, when the sun shines in through two corner windows. She slipped out of her silk-lined jacket. The action, lifting her breasts and opening her shirt, was unconscious or provocative—hard to tell.

'You mean May Ling,' she said. 'Who can blame him? She's very attractive and I was a bitch. I can see that now. It won't last.'

'You think you'll get him back?'

'Who knows?' She sipped again. 'This coffee's bitter.'

I grinned. 'Okay, I believe you're not jealous and now I know you're rational. I make lousy coffee. That's enough fencing—how do I find Malouf?'

'We.'

'You'd better explain.'

She pushed the coffee cup aside and drew in a breath. As at our first meeting, her hair was perfectly groomed and her makeup was expert. Her features in repose were unremarkable, but when she smiled or spoke the movement animated them and made her interesting to look at. Standish wouldn't have objected to her money, but it was easy to see why he would have been attracted to her even without it.

Her voice had a hard, determined edge. 'I'm not jealous about Miles anymore as I said, and it's not exactly jealousy I feel about Richard. I knew about the wife, of course, and I imagined there were other women, but May Ling's sister? Something sticks in my gullet about that—the way he used people.'

She waved her hand at the bookshelves. 'You read about people like that, but you don't expect to actually meet them. You don't expect to be one of the people who get used.'

'I'm not sure about that,' I said. 'You're from a privileged background, Felicity. I think you'll find that people from more ordinary circumstances get used all the time.'

She shook her head emphatically. 'No, they get exploited, sure. They're ill-treated, overlooked and ignored. But not *used* in the way Richard Malouf used me.'

She went on to tell me that in the full throes of her love affair with Malouf he'd asked her for a favour. He'd said he was negotiating an important business deal that involved convincing an investor that he knew about and understood the needs of children.

'It was something to do with persuading someone to sell a property for development on the understanding that there was to be recreation space for children. Richard told this man that he had two children, a boy and a girl. You can guess the rest.'

I said, 'I've been told about his charm, but . . .'

'Charm doesn't come anywhere near it. I allowed him to have a photograph taken of himself with my two. At that point I'd have done just about anything for him, short of harming the children, of course.'

I nodded.

'But I feel now as if I did harm them. I lied to them about who "that man" was and I came so close to saying "don't tell Daddy" it wasn't funny. Can you understand?'

'The level of deception? I think so. I've been told that Malouf may not even be his real name.'

She shrugged. 'Nothing'd surprise me. Well, when I was told that he'd died I sort of saw it as just part of a tragic love affair. Dramatised it for myself, I suppose.'

157

'But now?'

She laughed. 'The other day I walked past the development and guess what? No recreation area. I want to see Richard Malouf squirm.'

Malouf had a genius for leaving enemies in his wake. Easy to see, at least on a personal level, why he would've needed to fake his death. I couldn't be sure how many of the affairs he'd conducted with women overlapped, but one thing's for sure—you can't keep that many balls in the air forever. Felicity Pargetter was serious and had to be taken seriously.

'Where is he then?' I said.

'Oh no, we have to lay down the ground rules. I have to be there when you tackle him.'

I wasn't sure that I wanted to tackle him. Malouf was more than twenty years younger than me and soccer, sailing and golf had no doubt kept him fit, but I knew what she meant.

I drank the rest of my coffee, cold and bitter though it was, and pointed to the bookshelves. 'I've got a few of the same books as you—novels and true crime stuff. It's all very interesting but only some of it relates to what really happens. If you're thinking of barging in on this guy, forget it. He could be very dangerous. He might be very frightened.'

'I doubt that, but go on.'

'OK, you know him better than me. I only met him a couple of times. The point is, we'd have to establish for certain where he is and who might be with him. He might or might not be dangerous or frightened, but he's associated with some people who are very dangerous and not at all frightened. I bear the scars.'

'I see. Miles told me you'd been roughed up.'

I laughed. 'Is that what he called it? OK, he's paying, he can call it what he likes, but I plan to go very cautiously on the basis of your information. That's if I think it's credible. If he's there I'll think hard about what to do next and who with. And I'll have the say about how far along the road you travel.'

She threw back her head and laughed. 'You sound like John Howard—"we will say who comes to this county . . ."'

I groaned. 'Don't say that. Where d'you think he is?'

'You've shaken my confidence, but . . . Watsons Bay.'

20

She drove. Why not? Her Saab would make the trip quicker and more comfortably than my old Falcon. She was a good driver, more adventurous than May Ling but not foolhardy. Like most people, I'm anxious about being driven by someone else until I'm sure they're competent. She was and I relaxed. We didn't talk much until we reached Edgecliff. She glanced across as we passed Standish's office.

'Did he tell you about the trouble he's in?' I asked.

'A bit. Some nasty people putting pressure on him. I was surprised. One thing I'll say for Miles, for all his love of stars, he steered clear of the fashionable criminals.'

I knew what she meant: the ex-coppers and jailbirds who sponsored ghosted memoirs and invited the glitterati to the launches. The books mostly ended up on the remainder tables and the socialites didn't stick around when the day in the sun was done. I decided it was time to press her for a few details.

'Why Watsons Bay?'

'He had a boat.'

'We know that. His wife told us.'

She drove on for a while before she spoke again. 'What's she like?'

'Damaged, but recovering. Watsons Bay?'

'He used to pick me up in Double Bay and we'd sail up there. I love sailing.'

Unlike some others; that must've pleased him, I thought. This sounded promising. 'He had a mooring there?'

'No. He knew someone who had a mooring and he had the use of it sometimes, like the apartment.'

'The apartment?'

She steered smoothly around a truck. 'Look, the yacht was luxurious enough, everything that opened and shut, but the apartment was out of this world.'

'Hang on. Was the boat his?'

'Yacht. I don't know. He behaved as if it was.'

'Didn't it worry you? Someone working in a medium-range accountancy firm with all these toys?'

We passed the Gap and she didn't give the turn-off a glance. She wasn't the type.

'Ever been in love, Mr Hardy?'

'Cliff. Of course.'

'Did you size the person up completely before you knew you were that way?'

I thought of Cyn with her conservative North Shore

attitudes I hadn't probably seen and Helen Broadway with commitments to other people and other places that overrode her feelings for me.

'Point taken,' I said.

The sun broke through as we came down into Watsons Bay and the place took on the sparkle it advertises. They say the Isle of Capri is like that—you look across from cloudy Naples and see it out there under a patch of blue sky. I wouldn't know but I wouldn't mind taking a look.

I'd been to Watsons Bay for lunch in the pub beer garden or, if I was flush or someone else was paying, at Doyle's restaurant on the jetty. I'd also had a case fairly recently where one of the parties had used a gym in the area. I mentioned this to Felicity.

'There's a gym in the same street as the apartment block. Belle Vue it's called, would you believe?'

She turned into a street not far back from the water and drove slowly past a big four-level apartment complex, glowing white in the sunshine. The gym I'd mentioned was directly opposite. The apartments were obviously top of the range—large, with balconies big enough to accommodate a lot of greenery. She made a turn and we went down a narrow street beside the block. The corner apartments featured two balconies and views across the beach and the water all the way back to the city.

'Look up, top floor, of course,' Felicity said. 'On the corner. Multi-million dollar view.'

We completed the circuit and stopped below the complex.

'What's the security like?' I said.

She shrugged. 'I forget. I'm sorry . . . I didn't realise how coming back here would affect me. Shit—that bastard! I need a drink.'

And I needed to think. We went to the pub, sat under an umbrella with a bottle of wine and a seafood basket and watched the boats coming and going and the well-heeled people having a good time in the middle of the week. She dipped a chip in the tartare sauce, ate it and reached over to touch my hand.

'Why don't we just book a room and forget about all this?'

She burst into laughter as soon as she spoke. She'd had two glasses.

'I'm sorry,' she said. 'It's a line from a movie. I couldn't resist it.'

'What movie?'

'I forget.'

'How about the security?'

'I'm sorry, I really don't know. It was only a couple of times and I didn't notice.'

Something about the apartment block worried me, something half noticed. We finished the food and the wine, had coffee and walked on the beach for a while. Then we drove back and I saw what hadn't registered properly—a For Lease and a For Sale sign discreetly displayed at street level. The agent was local.

'Can you remember the number of the apartment?' I asked.

'Twenty.'

The estate agent—thirtyish, well-groomed, pearly white shirt —probably perked up when he saw the Saab stop outside. Could've felt a drop in spirits when he saw me but regained confidence at the sight of Felicity in her stylish clothes and her air of affluence. She said we were interested in the Belle Vue apartments.

'Bargains there,' he said, 'for leasing and buying. It's the GFC you see. Some of the owners took very hard hits.'

'Selling their boats,' I said.

'Indeed, and their apartments, though some have other homes, of course, and are leasing their places out here until things improve.'

'I like the look of the one at the top on the west corner,' Felicity said. 'Is it available?'

He gestured for us to sit while he went behind his desk and rummaged for a document. 'Here we are. Number 20. Yes, it's for sale.'

'How much?' I said.

'It'd be negotiable, dear,' Felicity said. 'Would it be vacant possession or is there a tenant?'

'It's vacant. Has been for some months. The owner, well, I have to be discreet, but he's very hard pressed. Would you like to see it?'

'Ball park figure,' I said.

He looked at me with dislike. 'Two million.'

I got to my feet. 'No way. We can do better.'

Felicity got up reluctantly. 'But . . .'

'No,' I said. 'Thanks for your time.'

'I'm sorry,' Felicity said.

We left. The rough diamond and the pearl.

We got in the car and she started the engine. 'I'm sorry, Cliff. A wild goose chase.'

'You know,' I said, 'under certain circumstances I reckon chasing wild geese could be fun.'

She laughed. 'I can see why Miles thinks so much of you. You can cope with things, can't you?'

'What else is there to do?'

Neither of us said much on the drive back. I asked her to drop me at a taxi rank. She pulled expertly into a tight spot, leaned across and kissed me on the cheek. Another one.

'I enjoyed today more than anything I've done for a while.

You've done me some good. I hope you find him and it all works out for you, Cliff.'

'Thanks. And for Miles?'

'Why not? Goodbye.'

21

The Watsons Bay dead end didn't depress me. Felicity had said it did her some good and the same was true for me. I'd enjoyed her company and her resilience struck a positive note with me. Too many of the people I've dealt with professionally have been diminished by their experiences. Felicity was a refreshing change. Money helps.

I had a quiet night and slept well. I woke up stiff, but forced myself to go to the gym. As often happens, I felt better once I started. I put in a solid workout and after a splash around in the spa I felt good. Good enough to face a solid breakfast at the Bar Napoli and shoot the breeze with the barista and some customers. As usual, it was sport and politics, although they're increasingly coming to look much the same.

The Balmain Tigers were offering a hundred grand commission to anyone who could find them a major sponsor. 'How about you, Mario?' a customer shouted, holding up the headline at the owner who'd drifted in as he did at whatever time pleased him.

'Ugly game. *Nessuna grazia, nessuna competenza.*'

I looked at Fortunato, known as Lucky, by the coffee machine. He shrugged. 'Means no grace, no skill.'

Not the place to argue with that. They went on to discuss the axing of the annual Norton Street Italian Festival by the local council. Not enough sponsors. It was something Lily and I had enjoyed. I missed her and I'll miss it.

I drove home feeling clear-headed, but without any fresh ideas about locating Richard Malouf. As it turned out I didn't need any. My mobile was ringing when I got through the door. I answered it.

'Hardy.'

'Mr Hardy, this is Richard Malouf.'

My hand tightened around the phone. ' Yes? Go on.'

'You'd be sceptical, naturally. You don't recognise my voice?'

'I only spoke to Malouf a couple of times. I don't remember anything about his voice.'

He went on to describe our meetings in Perry Hassan's office in precise detail, down to what we talked about. It was hard to see how anyone else could have had that information, but I wasn't buying it just yet. I asked a series of questions based on things Rosemary had told me and drew on some of the things Gretchen had said. I threw in a curly one about Felicity Pargetter and he fielded it neatly.

'OK,' I said. 'Suppose I believe you, what's the purpose of this call?'

'You've gone to a lot of trouble to find me. I'm impressed by your efforts. I thought you might want confirmation of my existence.'

'You're talking to yourself. If you're Malouf you're a target for people much more dangerous than—'

'Oh, I know that only too well. That's why I need your help. I siphoned off quite a bit of your money. It was only an exercise in proving to myself and others that it could be done, but still I can understand that you'd want it back. I can give you the precise figure if you like.'

I *was* convinced now. I remembered Malouf's cocky, self-satisfied manner more than his voice.

'So you're sitting somewhere on your boat tapping the keys with everything at your fingertips, is that right? I want the money back, sure, but there're two people dead and a few others very distressed and it all stems from you. You're the shit that hit the fan, or the fan itself, I'm not sure which.'

He laughed, still pleased with himself. 'Very graphic. I admit we've got a tangle here, but in my experience tangles can be . . . untangled. I think there's a way to do that.'

'Get you off the hook for killing the man who was identified as you?'

'Certainly. I admit I gave Selim the idea of pressuring Rosemary, but the detail's not important. That's not what I mean. I'm talking about a deal with the police to . . . absolve me of my . . .'

'Massive embezzlements.'

'If you want to put it that way, but believe me there's something very much bigger behind all this. Something global that would be of concern to every level of government in this country.'

Big talk, and probably rehearsed, but the trouble was he sounded as if he knew what he was talking about and I had just enough information to put flesh on the bones of what he was saying. I needed more, though.

I said, 'You've set up something big, got the ducks in a line, why not just run with it?'

No answer. I waited. 'Malouf?'

'Ah, good, you believe I'm who I say I am.'

'Fuck you. From everything I've heard, you're a lying, egotistical arsehole, so, yes, you've convinced me.'

I heard a sigh. 'Run with it, you say. I've been running with it. You can't imagine how hard I've worked. I'm tired.'

'You've done the dirty on Wong and Houli. You thought you could get away with that but now you have your doubts. I'm inclined to let you stew in your own juice.'

'That won't help you get your money back or stop your city from turning . . . cancerous.'

'What d'you mean?'

'That's the point—what do I mean? Talk to your principals. Talk to Inspector Chang and Sergeant Ali, talk to May Ling, but I'll tell you this—if Wong and Houli don't get a result soon they're going to feel some pressure and they'll destroy everyone in sight. I mean you, Standish, May Ling, Gretchen, Rosemary, Felicity, everyone! I'll be in touch.'

I didn't have the equipment set up to record phone calls any longer—I'd dismantled it some time after losing my PEA licence. I missed it now. I scribbled down as much as I could remember of what Malouf had said and wished I'd put some more questions to him. One would have been—how do you know so much about what I and others've been doing? There are ways of course, electronic methods, and it looked as though Malouf would be well up to speed on those, but the best method is to have someone on the inside keeping you informed.

I made a list of all the people Malouf had called my principals and scribbled notes beside the names—dates, brief details of character, attributes, meetings, likely motives. I had a lot of questions: were Chang and Ali all they appeared to be? Were Standish and May Ling consummate actors, playing both sides against the middle? What about Yusef Talat and Lester Wong? Could they be double-crossing their bosses? I didn't feel confident of these suspicions—too many gaps, too many breaks in the traffic. I looked at the list again and realised that I'd left one name off it—Richard Malouf. Maybe he wasn't sequestered on his high-tech boat; maybe he was out and about, monitoring all our activities. It was a thought, but I couldn't decide whether it was alarming or encouraging.

I needed an ally, someone to bounce ideas off and suggest strategies; someone to help. In the old days I would've turned to Frank Parker but I'd got him into trouble too many times before. Hank Bachelor was out; Megan had made it clear I wasn't to involve him in anything sticky. I looked at my list again—Sabatini. Why not?

I emailed Sabatini, setting out most of what I'd learned recently and telling him that Malouf had spoken to me. I knew that would hook him; no journalist can resist a Lazarus story. I implied that there was more to be said, and that I needed his expertise and possibly his hands-on help. A rock climber is a risk taker by definition, and Sabatini struck me as an ambitious type who probably had his mind on bigger things. Rosemary was definitely not a widow now, but there was a question as to whether she'd been legitimately married at all. I hinted at this. If their relationship was going full steam, what was more natural than that he'd want to be involved in dealing with the man who'd put her in danger?

I got an answer just an hour later. Sabatini didn't say where they were, but he'd been thinking about the Malouf business all the time and when he'd told Rosemary about my email she'd encouraged him to go back and help. I was reading the message when my mobile rang.

'Hardy, it's—'

I cut in. 'Be careful, there's a chance someone we know could be listening.'

'Shit, all right. She's safe with friends. I'm coming back. I'll be—'

'You'll be where you say you are when you get there.'

'OK.'

'Thanks. Think hard, we need ideas.'

'Can you give me anything more now? More to think about?'

'Yes, what is it that you most worry about?'

'Jesus, that's no help.'

'I know,' I said. 'Hurry back.'

22

I suppose I had some idea about Sabatini publishing something, maybe in his blog, and that drawing Malouf out into a meeting. Then we could hold him and either deal with the police or deal with Houli or Wong, whatever seemed to give the best result. It would depend on what he meant by 'cancerous', how serious the business they had set up really was.

It was a plan of sorts, an attempt to take the initiative. I didn't like the idea of just sitting around waiting for Dick Malouf to get in touch. When I'd mentioned the fact of the so far unknown dead man, he'd described it as an unimportant detail. Intelligence he undoubtedly had, and charm, to judge from the way he'd made himself appealing to women. That indifference to the life of another human being, though, also exhibited self-absorption. Just like Miles Standish, but worse. It was a serious weakness.

Most of the time I was comfortable in the house I'd lived in for many years, but occasionally the memories, good and bad, got to me and I needed to be somewhere else, preferably in company. I went down Glebe Point Road to the pub where I sometimes play pool but none of the people I play with was there. I had a drink and waited but no one I knew came in. I wandered off to an Italian restaurant where I could at least exchange pleasantries with the waiters and the owner. I was still down a few kilos and kept up the good work by ordering a salad, entrée-size lasagne and a small carafe of wine rather than a bottle. When eating alone I read. I had another Shipway title, *Free Lance*, with me; not as good as *Knight in Anarchy*, but interesting enough.

The restaurant had benches rather than chairs and as it filled up it was usual to have to share the space. I was enjoying the food and wine and interested in the book and didn't look as a man slid into the seat beside me.

'Good book?'

The last thing you want. I nodded, keeping my eyes on the page. I felt a sharp prick below my rib cage on the left side and my head swung round until I was looking into the eyes of Lester Wong.

'I can slip this into your heart in a fraction of a second, Hardy,' he said quietly. 'It'll kill you instantly and there wouldn't be much blood. I'd jump up in alarm as you slumped forward and that would be that. What do you think?'

There was blood already; I could feel it trickling down my

side. Lester wasn't looking at me now—just another customer waiting to order.

'Can I finish my dinner?'

'Of course. Take your time up to a point. We don't want to create a disturbance. Then you pay and we leave together.'

'You won't be able to keep the knife on me, Lester. I beat the shit out of you easily a while back and I could do it again.'

'Don't worry, I remember,' he said. 'But things are a bit different now. You see, we have May Ling in a car outside and if you cause any trouble we'll spoil her pretty face forever. Would you like to be responsible for that?'

I had weapons to hand: a knife, a fork, a glass and a carafe, usually enough to work with in a situation like this. But Wong's threat had that edge of menace that cut off all options. I put down the book and had a solid swig of the wine.

He took the knife away, leaving a small snick. The blood trickled a little harder. 'OK,' he said. 'That'll do. Let's go.'

It went smoothly. I was wearing a flannel shirt, jeans and a longish jacket; the blood was well concealed. Lester stayed close but managed to look as if he'd just changed his mind about eating there. We went out; Lester gestured at a people-mover parked close by and I saw May Ling through a window. Nobody took any notice as Lester escorted me towards the vehicle. A door slid open.

'Get in.'

Freddy Wong was sitting beside May Ling in the back row of seats. Lester pushed me towards the middle row.

'Any trouble?' Freddy said.

Lester said, 'Quiet as a lamb.' He said something in Chinese to the driver and the vehicle moved off.

'Say hello to your friend, Mr Hardy,' Freddy said.

May Ling said nothing. I could smell her perfume until Freddy lit a cigarette.

'What's the idea?' I said.

Freddy puffed smoke; May Ling coughed and he laughed. 'It's about Richard Malouf. What d'you think? You're going to tell me everything you know that will help me find him, or my beautiful cousin's face will be beautiful no longer.'

'He knows about the boat. I had to tell him,' May Ling said.

I could feel the blood congealing a bit north of my hip. With luck it'd soak through my pants and make a mess of the seat. 'It's all right,' I said. 'Has he got Gretchen?'

'Sunny?' Freddy said. 'No, but I will get her if necessary. Perhaps it won't matter, that's up to you.'

'We don't know where Malouf is,' I said.

Freddy opened a window and threw his butt out. 'We'll put that to the test. Just be quiet for a while and enjoy the ride.'

Broadway, George Street, Hay Street and into the heart of Chinatown. At street level a garage door in a large building opened electronically and we slid into a parking space big enough for half a dozen cars. It was already occupied by a sleek Alfa Romeo and a couple of working vehicles, a ute and a panel van.

We got out and Freddy ushered us towards an elevator. The driver came along as well—three of them and two of us. May Ling's hands were held together in front of her by plastic restraints. She wore the skirt of her suit and a blouse and looked cold.

I could feel, rather than see, Lester's knife close to my back. We went up three levels and came out in a short passage that led to what looked like a laboratory. Freddy guided May Ling into a chair by a bench and Lester shoved me towards a stool in a corner. The driver stood with his back to a wall.

'We used to knock up a bit of speed here,' Freddy said. 'It was good business for a time but the bikies made it tough after a while, especially the Lebos. A Lebo bikie is a mean bastard.'

'You'd know one,' I said.

Lester stepped forward and whacked me with a backhander. I saw it coming and eased back to reduce some of the force. It hurt, but delivering a solid backhander can throw you a bit off-balance and leave you open. It did, and I came at him with a heavy right to his ribs that sent him skittering. He raised the knife and the driver moved forward with his hands in a martial arts position.

'That's enough!' Freddy snapped. 'Settle down, Hardy. There's no need for this. We're talking and dealing here, I hope.'

He opened a cabinet over the bench and took out a couple of bottles and a beaker. He unscrewed the tops from the bottles and poured a little from one and a little from the other into the beaker. The mixture fizzed and gave off a wisp of smoke with an acrid smell.

'Now, this won't kill her. It won't even cause her to faint if I know May Ling, but it'll eat away at her skin and tissue beyond repair by any plastic surgeon.'

May Ling screamed. The sound went through me like a dentist's drill hitting a nerve. I jerked up and Lester flicked the knife across inches from my face.

'Good reactions,' Freddy said, 'very satisfactory. Now, I want to know everything, down to the last detail.'

There was nothing else to do. I told Freddy absolutely everything I knew about Richard Malouf and his involvement and Houli's. My phone call from Malouf was news to May Ling but she didn't react. Her eyes were focused on the beaker of acid. I left out where Rosemary and Gretchen were but nothing else. He listened carefully, stopping me only a couple of times with questions. Freddy was a very intelligent man, and one with long experience of applying pressure and assessing the results.

When I'd finished he spoke in Chinese to Lester and the driver and then turned his attention back to me. He moved the beaker away on the bench. 'One phone call only?'

'That's right.'

'Did he say when he'd call again?'

'No.'

'It seems we'll have to keep you alive.'

'For now,' Lester said.

Freddy smiled. 'It depends on how it all works out. D'you know what Chou En-Lai said when he was asked what he thought were the results of the French Revolution?'

I shook my head. I moved on the stool to get more comfortable and winced as my shirt came away from where it had been stuck by congealed blood to the cut.

'He said it was too soon to tell. That's how things stand now. It's too soon to tell, but you have certain things in your favour.'

'You'll let May Ling go?'

He laughed. 'That's another thing it's too soon to tell about. Now, what did you plan to do next, after you'd finished your cheap little dinner?'

I hadn't told him any more than that Malouf wanted to do a deal with the police, nothing about Sabatini. 'I was thinking about it when Lester stuck his knife into me,' I said. 'I was going to get in touch with Inspector Chang and try to set something up, act as a go-between, I guess.'

'You'd be happy to see Malouf get clear in return for destroying me and Selim Houli?'

I shrugged. 'I doubt it'd work out quite like that, but it's too soon to tell.'

I heard an angry grunt from Lester and got ready for another blow but Freddy laughed and raised his hand placatingly. 'Touché. Well, we'll just have to play along with you and Malouf, but I think we'll keep the police out of it. That's not to say you won't tell Malouf that you've contacted them. You're going to have to do a bit of acting.'

'You'll have to let me tap Malouf for some information as to what it's all about. He'd expect I'd need something more to get Chang interested.'

'You're right. I almost like you, Hardy; you're not completely dumb. You still want to understand things. I respect that. I'll have to try to make sure you don't learn so much that we have to kill you.'

'Try to make sure Lester understands that.'

An angry burst of Chinese from Lester made May Ling raise her head and shoot him a look of loathing.

Freddy lit a cigarette. 'Lester and I don't quite see eye to eye on this. I try not to kill people. It's bad for business.'

For the first time, May Ling spoke. 'You're killing Sunny, you creep.'

'Business,' Freddy said.

I said, 'What about Houli?'

'What about him?'

'Whatever this is, you're in it together.'

Freddy reached out for an empty beaker on the bench and drew it towards him. He dropped ash into it. 'So far,' he said, 'so far.'

23

I'd left Freddy with the impression that Malouf was on his boat which I didn't think was necessarily the case. He barked instructions to the driver who left in a hurry. At a guess he was going to try to find the boat, and as no one had had any luck at that so far, it didn't seem likely he would. Freddy picked his butt out of the beaker and dropped it in the acid. At the smoke and smell May Ling shrank back in her chair.

'Little reminder,' Freddy said. 'Lester, get his phone.'

I know less than nothing about satellites and electronic tracking, but I could see what was in Freddy's mind. He'd have someone try to track the source of Malouf's call when it came and be able to take the initiative. May Ling and I would be expendable. I thought Malouf would have found a way to prevent a trace but Freddy didn't know that. Maybe Freddy was reluctant to kill but Lester wasn't. Just at that moment, the phone was an asset. I took it from my pocket and juggled it as Lester moved towards me with his knife.

'No phone, no trace,' I said. I tossed it up and caught it.

Lester glanced at Freddy and that was my chance. I kicked Lester as hard as I could in the crotch. He yelled, dropped the knife and both his hands went down protectively. I head-butted him; he went down and I kept moving. Freddy had the brains but not the moves. He was frozen for just a little too long. I pinned him back against the bench and grabbed the beaker of acid. Blood was streaming from Lester's forehead, but he recovered and crawled towards the knife.

'No!' I held the beaker at Freddy's shoulder.

Lester stopped. 'You wouldn't.'

I jiggled the beaker. The acid hissed. 'Try me.'

The blood was running into his eyes, blinding him. He rubbed at his face with his sleeve and swore in English and then in Chinese.

'May Ling,' I said, 'get the knife.'

She didn't move.

'Get the fucking knife!'

She pushed up from the chair and strode across the floor. She bent in one fluid motion for the knife and glided close to where I still had Freddy gasping for breath and watching the acid. She shoved the knife hard into his soft belly and had to use an upward ripping motion to pull it out. Freddy screamed and sagged towards her. She fended him off with the hand holding the knife and the blade went in again. I let him go and he fell to the floor with blood gushing over May Ling's high heel shoes. I took the knife from her hand.

It was a big knife, like the one in the movie *Jagged Edge*, and I knew how sharp it was. May Ling had dug it in deep, and it must have done drastic internal damage to Freddy because he was dead within a minute. Lester, still dripping blood himself, cradled his brother's head in his lap and wept.

May Ling and I left the room, took the lift to the ground floor and walked out of the building into the crowded street. As soon as the cold air hit her she began to tremble. I pulled her closer to the building line and put my arms around her.

'I murdered him.'

'He was a vicious bastard. He would have scarred you and Gretchen too if things hadn't pleased him. He had it coming.'

We stood until she stopped trembling and signalled that she was ready to move. I kept my arm around her shoulders and gasped once when her elbow nudged the cut in my side.

'What?'

'Lester cut me. Just a scratch.'

'You got more than you bargained for when you came to see Miles that day, Cliff. Didn't you?'

'So did you.'

Wrong thing to say: it set her off again and she almost stumbled and started to sob quietly. I steered her slowly up Hay Street through a thick press of people out to shop, eat, have a good time. Her shoes and feet were covered in blood. I hailed a taxi in George Street and sat beside her in the back.

'Glebe,' I said to the driver.

'Where?' she said.

'You're coming to my place.'

She nodded and slumped back in the seat. Would the driver see blood on the floor when he cleaned the cab? Maybe. Would he do anything about it? Again, maybe. I stopped the cab in Glebe Point Road. No point in leaving a clear trail to the house.

I got her there. She was calm. She took off her shoes and stockings and I gave her a damp towel to clean her feet. The head butt had set up a ringing in my damaged ear. I stripped off my clothes, cleaned the cut with alcohol swabs and applied a dressing. I put on fresh clothes and joined her. Her usually immaculate hair was untidy and there were strain lines beside her eyes and mouth. She was still beautiful, but she'd never quite wear that imperturbable expression again.

I made coffee and we drank it laced with Black Douglas scotch rather than Courvoisier. She sat quietly for a while, nursing her cup. She looked around the room, taking in the books, CDs, photos and general air of careless maintenance. There were magazines and newspapers lying around and a glass and a coffee mug on a bookshelf. The carpet was new but hadn't seen a vacuum cleaner for a while.

When she seemed to be more or less composed, I said, 'Where did they pick you up?'

'At my place. Freddy . . . he helped me find it and lent me some of the money. I didn't know he had a key. I suppose I should have. What's going to happen now? Were you going to tell Miles about Malouf contacting you?'

I liked that about her, not having the first thought immediately for herself. I said I wasn't sure and that I'd have to think things through again now that Freddy was out of the picture.

'What about Lester?'

'I don't think he amounts to much without Freddy, do you?'

She shook her head. Mention of Freddy raised the inevitable question. 'Are you going to tell the police what happened?'

'I don't see why. Lester's going to cover it up in some way, and as far as I'm concerned it was a kind of self-defence.'

'Thank you. Oh God, what about the knife?'

'It's in the pocket of my jacket. Tomorrow it'll be in the sludge at the bottom of Blackwattle Bay.'

I showed her the spare room and found her a clean T-shirt. She kissed me on the cheek. When beautiful young women kiss you on the cheek you know you're over the hill, but I didn't really feel like that. As Wesley said, I still had some moves.

I took some pills. The pain in my side eased and the ringing in my ear dulled down. I thought about May Ling's knife work as I drifted off to sleep. She didn't owe him money anymore.

191

24

Standish collected May Ling in the morning. I brought him up to date on the recent events and told him that Freddy Wong had been killed by accident, with no likely repercussions for May Ling or me. She had regained complete control of herself by then, had showered, used my comb and didn't look any the worse for not having any makeup. She'd washed and rinsed her stockings and cleaned her shoes. Looked just about ready to go to work. Standish was all protective solicitude. He was relieved to hear that one of the people threatening him was out of the picture. I wondered what he'd think about his lover if he'd seen the way she'd stuck it to Freddy.

'Thanks again, Hardy. What now?'

'I have to think. As I said, the Wongs were all set to double-cross Houli. I'm going to try to find a way to make use of that.'

'Surely you just go to the police now and tell them Malouf's alive and leave it to them to catch him?'

'Don't you want to know what it's all about?'

'Not really, no.'

'I do,' May Ling said.

That wrong-footed Standish and he buckled straight off. 'Do what you have to do,' he said. He must have thought that sounded limp so he added, 'Do you need any more money?'

I said I didn't. May Ling wanted to visit Gretchen to make sure she was all right. Standish seemed to think that was an excellent idea. I told them to be careful, to keep close to other people and lock the doors.

'I think we might take a short holiday,' Standish said. 'But you have the mobile number in case you need any help.'

'Maybe a harbour cruise,' I said, 'or a houseboat on the Hawkesbury. Keep a lookout for Malouf.'

May Ling laughed.

'You've got a sick sense of humour, Hardy,' Standish said.

They left. I thought May Ling might give me another peck on the cheek but she didn't.

Sabatini rang. 'Airport. Want to pick me up?'

'In the bar,' I said.

He was nursing a beer when I arrived. No sign of jet lag. I got a Hahn Lite and we went to a quiet corner. I started to speak but he stopped me, reached into his bag and pulled out a tape recorder.

'Okay?'

I thought about it and decided it wouldn't hurt to have a record of events—things said and speculations made. I gave him chapter and verse while he finished his drink. He stopped the recording while I got two more. As I crossed to the bar I couldn't help thinking about Richard Malouf and his apparent awareness of the movements of some of the players—Standish, May Ling and me. I looked around, but there was no one answering his description, unless he was a master of disguise.

Resuming, I got to where the Wongs had picked up May Ling and me and there I did a bit of editing, much as I had for Standish. But Sabatini was a journalist.

'So who killed him?'

'It was a kind of accident.'

'Bullshit.'

'I was there, you weren't.'

'You don't trust me.'

'Look, the situation is fluid. At some point we're going to have to deal with the police. We'll be trying to hold the best hand we can, exert the most leverage. We don't need to give anyone ammunition, anything they can use to apply . . . opposite pressure. Shit, I'm talking like a physicist.'

'This tape is my professional property. I'm a working journalist. I don't have to make its contents available to anyone.'

I shook my head. 'That's what the book says, but you know and I know that the right judge in the right court can put you in gaol and the police can paint any picture of you they like with the cooperation of your press colleagues. Ever been busted for pot? Pros? Ever up on a DUI? Go through your accountant's work on your tax with a fine-tooth comb, do you? Make sure every claim is kosher? You know how it works.'

Sabatini turned off the recorder. 'Tell me off the record.'

I finished my beer: two lights in an hour. Probably all right to drive, but best to wait a while.

I said, 'When it's over. Maybe. But don't worry, you'll get your story.'

He had to be content with that and we got down to planning how to draw Richard Malouf out into the open and what to do after that.

'Why not tell the police that he's still alive, wait for his call and get them to trace it?'

'No,' I said, 'from what I've been told about him and from what he said himself, he'd take very good precautions against that.'

'Then do as he says, broker a deal with the police.'

'They wouldn't be in it. That's one of things worrying me. He's not playing the game he says he is. He can't really imagine the police would let him go, even if the business he's involved in is huge and he's in the clear on the two deaths.'

'Why not?'

'Too hard to cover up. Too many favours to call in at too high a level. No, we need to get hold of him ourselves and dictate the terms.'

'How?'

'How d'you squeeze information out of people who don't want to give it?'

He looked uncomfortable. 'I wouldn't put it quite like that, but one technique is to put pressure on someone else, someone the subject cares about. Who does Malouf care about?'

'On the face of it, only himself, but I'm wondering. Houli told Rosemary that Malouf wasn't his real name, remember? If we could find out what his real name is, *who* he is, we might get somewhere.'

'Jesus, that's a big ask, but . . .'

'What?'

'I remember when I was researching him, when I thought he was dead, I came across some anomaly, something that didn't quite fit. I dismissed it and I can't remember now what it was, but there was something. I'd have to go through my files.'

'Where are they?'

He reached into his pocket and took out a memory stick attached to his keys. I pointed to the overnight bag at his feet.

'Is your laptop there, your notebook, or whatever?'

'No, I left it with Rosemary. Anyway I'd have to go to my computer at home because it's all encrypted, the software . . .'

'Don't tell me, I wouldn't understand. Let's go.'

In the Coogee flat, Sabatini dumped his bag and went straight to the computer in his workroom. He had it up and running in a split second and began tapping the keys, wiping boxes and scrolling at a rapid rate the way they do.

'Here it is, look.'

On the screen was a photograph of a school soccer team. The boys looked to be about sixteen or seventeen and wore that confident expression that goes with private school and sporting prowess. The names of the players were listed at the bottom of the photograph. Sabatini pointed. A tall, dark haired youth stood in the back row and a smaller, less dark boy was in the middle row. According to the list of names the smaller boy was Richard Malouf and the taller was William Habib.

Sabatini put his finger on the boy in the back row. 'That's Malouf without a doubt, or the man we know as Malouf.'

I peered. 'They're alike, but you're right.'

'I sort of noticed it when I was working on this stuff but I just put it down to a glitch in the names. I should've checked. Now that there's some doubt about Malouf's identity . . .'

'When I've run up against a name change or confusion,' I said, 'I always check the dates. How do the dates we know about him stack up?'

Sabatini worked through his notes and his published pieces.

'The football photo is of their last year at school. If he did a four-year honours course at WA there's a three-year gap between leaving school and going to university.'

'I've heard of a gap year, but not three years. We need to find out more about William Habib. The starting point's the school.'

Sabatini sighed. 'I'll try. I need some coffee. Would you mind? The milk's probably off, though.'

'I'll leave you to it.' There was plenty of ground coffee in the kitchen but the milk smelt dodgy. I was glad to get out into the fresh beachside air.

Coogee is hilly, good cardiac exercise territory. I tramped up a few hills and finished at the shops in Clovelly Road. I bought the milk and a bottle of wine and some sandwiches. Who knows how long an Internet search takes? Could be hours, so I bought a paper as well and looked at the headlines on the way back. The news about the economy was good— things that should be up were up and things that should be down were down. The government was happy; the opposition was grumpy. The experts were puzzled.

Sabatini was clattering away, swearing occasionally and muttering to himself. He had some classical music I didn't recognise playing softly; no surprise there, I can only recognise 'Bolero' and a couple of Beethoven concertos, a bit of Tchaikovsky at a pinch. I made the coffee and took a mug and a sandwich in to him.

'Thanks,' he said, with his eyes on the screen.

'How's it going?'

'Takes time.'

I went out onto the balcony to drink my coffee and look at the water. Many times I've been tempted to move to the eastern suburbs, get a flat with a view, swim eight months a year. Something holds me back.

I heard Sabatini's printer chattering—a good sign. I finished the coffee, opened the bottle of wine and drank some with a sandwich. A greyish morning had given way to a bright afternoon. I read some more of the paper and dozed in the sun.

'We've come up with something.'

I jerked awake as Sabatini came out onto the balcony with a sheaf of printout in his hand.

'I got on to the school, Riverside Grammar. They have the students' outstanding results over the last twenty odd years and Richard Malouf is right up there. No sign of William Habib. Same for sporting achievements and there the position is reversed. Malouf OK at soccer; Habib good at everything.'

He flicked through the sheets. 'A Richard Malouf died in Cooktown Hospital in 1992. A drowning. The school has him listed as a departed old boy. A brief report in the *Cooktown Courier* says he was accompanied on the swim by an unnamed school friend who failed to save him.'

Sabatini held up another sheet. 'A Richard Malouf enrolled at the University of Western Australia in 1994.'

'I wondered about that,' I said. 'When you've been a star at a Brisbane private school why do you go to uni in Western Australia? It's a long way to go to get away from home.'

Sabatini went on. 'This Malouf didn't do so flash except at computer stuff. He was brilliant at that. But he captained the soccer team and was the opener for the cricket team; handy pace bowler, too.'

'Sounds more like Habib. Any trace of him and why the switch?'

'William Habib was charged in 1990 for assault with intent to do grievous bodily harm. He never appeared in court. Bail was posted and forfeited. This is the kicker—Selim Houli put up the bail.'

We talked around that for a while. It looked as if William Habib had assumed the identity of Richard Malouf and had gone as far away as he could to gain his credentials using Malouf's school results to get him started. Then he worked his way back east and found himself a spot where he could gain access to a lot of business accounts and manipulate others, under cover of legitimate activity with Selim Houli as some kind of backer.

'It leaves us no closer to finding out what the big picture is,' Sabatini said.

'No, but at least we know something about him that he doesn't know we know. Tell me William Habib has an old mother who he couldn't bear to see troubled.'

'I checked the Brisbane phone directory. There's a column and a half of Habibs.'

'I wonder if he killed Malouf and swiped some of the things he'd need to do the identity change.'

Sabatini shrugged. 'It was a long time ago.'

It was a stalemate; far from learning anything that might give us the initiative, we were simply waiting for Malouf/ Habib to contact me when he chose. We decided that the only thing to do was wait a few days for the call and play it by instinct at that point—perhaps hinting that we knew his real identity and hoping that might throw him off-balance.

'If he doesn't call in that time?' Sabatini asked.

'You write something along the lines of "Is Richard Malouf still alive? And who is he?" Something like that and see if it touches a nerve.'

'The police'll pick up on that and they'll be after us.'

'The more the merrier. I've dealt with the police before.'

'Yeah, and lost your licence. But, okay, we'll see how it plays out. I owe you for Rosemary. Keep your phone charged up.'

We had a drink and left it at that. I drove back to Glebe. The roadwork that had been going on for almost a year was almost finished and some of the businesses that had looked to be struggling were picking up. I reckoned it was about time I saw Megan again and was thinking about that as I turned into my street. The low winter sun was in my eyes and I shielded them with my hand as I brought the car to a stop outside my house. I was still a bit dazzled when I got out and jiggled my keys, feeling for the right one.

'Hardy!'

Lester Wong stepped out from behind one of the shrubs in front of the house. The muzzle of his sawn-off shotgun was about three metres from my chest.

A voice: 'Police! Drop the gun!'

I hit the ground hard. There was a roar like an unmuffled exhaust, and shredded leaves dropped on me as I heard the pellets bouncing off the car.

'Drop it!'

Two sharp cracks, and when I looked up I saw Lester on his back, sprawled across the tiled path and he wasn't moving.

part three

25

I had grazed palms, bruised knees and torn trousers—pretty soft landing after facing a sawn-off. That didn't mean I could go quietly inside and pour myself a congratulatory drink. The police arrived, then the media; mobile phone signals bounced around and I ended up in Chang's Surry Hills office.

'Thought it was about time we had a chat, Hardy,' Chang said. 'Lucky for you we were there, or lucky Ali was there— best pistol shot in the service.'

Ali was still wearing his displeased expression.

'Thank you,' I said.

'You might like to help me with the paperwork.'

'We're getting whispers that Freddy Wong's not around, and now his crazy brother comes after you. We also know Sabatini flew back home today.'

'Is this a formal interview?'

'No, come on, Hardy. You're up to your balls in something too big for you. I had to talk fast to keep DI Caulfield off your case—being present at two violent deaths tends to make people suspicious. Sheer stroke of luck that now you're not just down the way from your place in the bloody morgue.'

All true, and Malouf/Habib hadn't rung. Maybe he wouldn't. Maybe Lester's death, which was bound to be on the news that night, would scare him off. When I thought about it, our plan for something Sabatini could write was our best chance of provoking him and that would bring the police running anyway. It was time to come clean—well, cleanish.

I told them Freddy Wong was definitely dead, and that three people (that was stretching it a bit) whom I wouldn't name were present. I said it was somewhere between an accident and self-defence.

Ali shot an astonished look at Chang. 'Can you believe this guy?'

'There's more,' I said.

I told them that a man calling himself Richard Malouf had spoken to me on the phone, the deal he'd proposed and that he said he'd be in touch. I said that I was working with Sabatini and that we'd uncovered evidence to suggest that his real name was William Habib. I started to talk about the plan Sabatini and I had, but Ali cut me off with a snort of derision and an angry slap of his hand against the wall.

Chang, making notes, fiddled with his pen. 'You didn't think to get in touch with us when you got this call?'

'Thought about it, but, no, I didn't.'

'Why not?' Ali snapped.

'I got into this to try to get a couple of gangsters off the back of a client . . .'

'You don't have the right to have a fucking client,' Chang said.

'A certain person, then. To help someone in a difficult situation.'

'And recover the money Malouf stole from you,' Ali said.

I shrugged. 'If it worked out that way, sure. But that's not the real reason.'

Ali shook his head. 'All right, what is?'

I knew. It was to do with a missing person, a false identity, something unknown at the heart of the matter. And it was about doing something I'd been doing for a long time and was good at; about not feeling useless. But it was difficult to put all that into words.

'Curiosity,' I said.

Ali walked out of the room.

Chang leaned back in his chair. 'What am I going to do with you? Cancerous—that was the word he used, right?'

'Right.'

'What does it mean?'

'It's a metaphor.'

'I know it's a fucking metaphor. So?'

I shrugged. 'Something that'll eat . . . away at society.'

'Doesn't cancer sort of overwhelm the other cells in the body?'

'I think you're right. Whatever it refers to it's something very big. He sounded serious. I've been thinking about you and the sergeant: a special unit to combat Chinese and Lebanese crime? There have to have been whispers, signs of something brewing. Look, without giving you the details, Freddy Wong was prepared to do something horrific to another person just to get some information. And this Malouf/Habib—he knows what's going on, he has a connection to Houli and is prepared to double-cross him. That takes guts and it suggests that the business, whatever it is, has got too big, is getting out of control.'

Chang glanced down at the notes he'd been scribbling while I talked. 'Tell me again about this deal.'

I went over it but I'd remembered another detail.

'He knew your name and the name of your bad-tempered mate—not that I'm not grateful to him for saving my life.'

'But he hasn't called you back. We can't find any trace of that boat. It could be registered in Panama or Tuvalu, where they don't give a shit about any rules or regulations.'

'He knew too much about our movements to be some-where offshore. He's around, watching, listening, waiting.'

'So he could know that you're here, talking to me?'

I said nothing but I looked at the door Ali had slammed behind him.

Chang closed his eyes. Without those keen eyes enlivening

his face he looked older, more weary. 'He's a good man. He saved your life.'

'He shot a Chinaman. Where did he get him?'

'Head and heart.'

'Head to kill; heart to be sure. Would he shoot a Malouf or a Habib?'

'You're a pain in the arse, Hardy,' Chang said, 'undermining the integrity of a trusted officer.' He looked at his notes again. 'He cut you off when you started to talk about your plan with Sabatini. If he's . . . on the other side, why wouldn't he want to hear all about that?'

'Because he wouldn't want *you* to hear about it, and he *would* want to catch me on my own.'

Chang glanced around the room as if help could be found in the filing cabinets, the bookshelves, the citations on the walls. There's no help there as we both knew: it comes down to decisions, guesses, risks to be taken. I knew then, as I'd always known, that he was a good man who'd put the right thing to do up at the top of his agenda. But I had to give him a nudge.

'Stephen,' I said, 'I couldn't help noticing that you wrote your notes on our interview in Chinese characters. Do you always do that?'

'Sometimes,' he said. 'Just sometimes.'

Chang called Ali back and we discussed the plan to provoke Malouf/Habib through an article Sabatini would write and post as a blog. We also talked about the possibility of striking a deal with Malouf/Habib in exchange for his exposing the grand scheme.

'Cowboy stuff,' Ali said. 'We can't guarantee immunity or anything like that.'

'Why not?' I said. 'You've done it before.'

Chang nodded. 'True, but by Jesus the information better be good.'

I said, 'He'll want details and help—a passport probably, maybe money, maybe a hostage.'

'You seem to know a lot about his thinking,' Ali said.

'I'm just putting it together how I'd want it if it was my way out. If what he can reveal is as big as he says, he'll have to run a long, long way.'

Chang smiled. 'And not to Hong Kong or the Emirates. Where would you guess, Karim?'

I studied Ali closely. Was he thinking about how to deliver this information to Malouf/Habib, or were our suspicions all wrong? Impossible to tell; his handsome face was set in its customary sceptical expression when I was in the picture. He shrugged. 'South America.'

'Right,' I said. 'Brazil. The new Ronnie Biggs. The difficult part is to get a hint in Sabatini's piece that the police are considering a deal. Just a hint.'

'This is bullshit,' Ali said. 'I vote we round up Houli and Talat and tell them what we know and get them to tell us what this is all about. Do a deal with them if we must and fuck Malouf . . . or whatever his name is.'

Chang looked at me. 'Hardy?'

'It's not a bad idea, but my guess is after what happened to the Wong boys, Houli and Talat will be very hard to find.'

Ali pulled out his mobile phone, wandered off to the other side of the room and made some calls. His responses were negative grunts.

Closing the phone, he said, 'I hate to admit it, but you're right—they're lying very low.'

Chang looked down at the characters on his notepad. 'Well, this looks like the only game in town, but I'm warning you, Hardy, you contact us the second you hear from Malouf. I'm calling him that until I learn otherwise. Try playing some independent smartarse game and you'll have your next heart bypass in gaol.'

Ali liked that; it was the first time I'd seen him smile.

26

What we were proposing wasn't really all that unusual or outrageous. There were journalists virtually embedded with the various police forces and intelligence agencies, and others who were leaked to systematically and operationally. There was a recent case where someone on the police or the intelligence strength had leaked to a paper about a planned raid on terrorist suspects. The paper did a deal with the operations leader not to publish until the raid was underway. Somehow the story got into print early, and the raid had to be moved forward. Things in that kind of world can go seriously wrong.

The only substantial contribution to Sabatini's blog I made was the headline:

IS RICHARD MALOUF STILL ALIVE?

Readers will remember the case of the financial wizard Richard Malouf who managed to spirit away millions of dollars from his clients' accounts, lose it gambling with figures in the Sydney underworld, and, apparently, die from a gunshot wound in his car. Suicide or murder? The coronial inquiry has yet to sit.

But it may be none of these things. Try faked death. A source close to a certain police task force investigating crime in the Chinese and Lebanese communities has told this writer that Malouf may still be alive. No details are available, other than that there have been as yet unverified 'sightings'. More intriguing are hints that Malouf may not be the real name of the man in question. Questions to be answered: is he alive? If so, who was the dead man in the car and who killed him? And why does this writer get the feeling that in the minds of certain police there are bigger fish to fry than financial juggler, lothario and crack sportsman Richard 'Dicky' Malouf?

Sabatini sent me a draft of the article and I complimented him on it. I'd briefed him fully on my interview with Chang and Ali and I felt he'd struck the right notes.

'You realise,' he said, 'that if your suspicions about this Sergeant Ali are right, it won't matter. Malouf will know exactly how the land lies.'

'When and if he rings I'll try to trip him up on that.'

'What if he doesn't ring?'

'I think he will. People can only play a double game for so long. He might feel safer now that Freddy Wong's out of action but he might not. There could be someone worse in the wings. Same with Houli and Talat; he might think the stakes have gone up for them. A deal with the police, a version of witness protection, not that he'd be willing to bear witness, is his best chance.'

'If the cops play it straight. D'you think they will?'

'No. We have to be on our toes and it gets very complicated if Ali's dirty. Are you worried about getting your story?'

'No. I'm worried about Rosemary. She wants to come back.'

'Tell her not yet.'

'I have.'

'Insist.'

'How much luck have you had at insisting a woman do something she doesn't want to do?'

I told him to be careful, lock his door, stay in company and keep the instant backup number Chang had given me close to hand. It didn't seem likely that Houli would come after us, but it was possible. And Malouf/Habib himself might not make the quiet approach he'd spoken of. We still only had his word that he wasn't involved in the death of the substitute. And what of his school chum on a lonely beach in the far north?

I got a call-waiting signal and rang off, after promising Sabatini I'd contact him immediately if it was our man. It wasn't.

'Cliff,' Megan said, 'what the hell have you been up to?'

Is that what it comes to—your children addressing you the way your parents did?

'The usual,' I said.

'I saw the news and I recognised the house and the Falcon and that was you being bundled into the police car with the coat over your head. Did you shoot that man?'

'No, he shot at me but he missed.'

'You didn't say anything about the case you were on involving men with shotguns.'

'Don't tell me I'm too old for it. I was too old for shotguns twenty years ago. We're all too old for shotguns. There were developments, changes. Things got heavier. The car's a bit of a mess; those pellets bugger up the duco.'

She let out an exasperated sigh. 'Fuck the car. Anyway, you're not up on a charge or anything?'

'No.'

'Is it still dangerous?'

'Could be, but don't worry, I've got allies.'

'You once told me to be wary of allies because they tended to be balanced by enemies.'

'Did I? That sounds glib.'

'It is, but it's good glib. Well, I wanted to tell you that you should call on Hank if you need help. I know I'm going back on what I said before, but I really don't want to be one of those women who stop men from doing what they want to do. I can tell that Hank's bored with the routine stuff and when he saw the news he lit up. He was energised. I prefer him like that and I told him so. Just take care, Cliff, and come and see us when you can.'

'I will. How's everything going?'

'He's kicking.'

'He?'

'Yep, a boy, and he just gave me a bloody great thump.'

Malouf/Habib rang me at noon precisely the following day.

'You took your time,' I said, 'Richard, or is it William?'

He chuckled. 'You've done some homework.'

'Me and others. What made you decide to call? I thought you might have given up on the idea.'

'No, you didn't think that or anything like it. Never mind why, we're here now.'

So much for my notion about tripping him up.

'The police are interested in a deal,' I said, 'under certain conditions, naturally.'

'Naturally, and you're authorised to speak for them? I find that hard to believe.'

'Just at this initial stage, to set the rules, then it'll be out of my hands.'

'Okay, what're the conditions?'

I'd thrashed this out thoroughly with Chang and Ali, trying to guess not only what Malouf/Habib would accept, but what he'd anticipate in a negotiation. I wanted to avoid police-speak, but still get the flavour of a police arrangement across.

'First, the name of the man identified as you, and some evidence that you didn't kill him.'

'Go on, I'm jotting this down.'

So to speak, I thought. I could hear his fingers on a keyboard.

'A solid indication of what this is all about. Some explanation of the word you used—cancerous.'

'Mmm, and . . .?'

'That's all for now. They'll want hard evidence, documents, emails, banking details, photographs, whatever, to back up what you say. Hard evidence against Selim Houli.'

The self-satisfied chuckle again. 'Not against Freddy Wong?'

I had to be careful that he didn't lead me into places I wasn't prepared for.

'The police assume you're talking about organisations. They know Freddy Wong had connections far and wide. They assume you'll have . . . relevant information about others.'

'Who killed Freddy?'

The question caught me off-guard and I almost answered. I stopped myself and simply said that I wasn't at liberty to say, but he got something out of my hesitation.

'I'm guessing you were there and that's why nutty Lester came after you. I'm guessing May or Sun Ling.'

'Guess away.'

That was a nugget for me—he didn't know where Sun Ling was, but he did know something about them. The more I heard from him the more I formed the opinion that he was a very dangerous man. There was something objective, analytical, about everything he said, as if he were attempting to anticipate two or three moves ahead and come out on top.

'I assume you're recording this, Hardy?'

I was. Chang had given me the equipment, but I didn't respond.

'You would be. That's good. There's no point in trying to trace the call though. This phone'll soon be . . .'

'At the bottom of the harbour?'

He laughed. 'Good try. I'll be brief and try to satisfy your conditions. The dead man was what you might call an undocumented person. He was a Lebanese relative of mine I . . . introduced into the country. He was working with me on this project until about the time I decided to go, as it were, freelance. Lester Wong killed him thinking he was me.'

'That's hard to prove, given that Lester's dead.'

'I can back it up, at least part of the way.'

Slippery, I thought, *very slippery*.

'As for the other conditions, I'll give you some names and let your . . . principals make what they will of them: Harvey Dong, Ah Pin, Mustafa Khalid and . . . let's say, Grant Simmonds.'

I said, 'That's not much to go on,' but I was talking to myself. He'd hung up.

I met Chang in Burton Place, the square down a level from Oxford Street. I had Googled the names and got results for three of them, not Grant Simmonds. I told him about the call and passed my printouts to him.

He stirred sugar into the long black he'd ordered and ignored the papers. 'You didn't get a hint about his source of information . . . locally?'

'Not a clue. He's very smart. You heard the recording, the one time I tried to trick him he was onto it like a shot.'

'He says Lester killed the mystery man?'

'Yeah, and that he can back it up. To use his words, "in part".'

'I found it hard to listen to; it sounded as if he played you like a fish.'

'I doubt you'd have done any better.'

He pulled the sheets towards him and looked through them as he stirred his coffee. He was seeing that Harvey Dong and Ah Pin were Hong Kong criminals, the heads of gangs within the Triad structure. Mustafa Khalid was the leader of a Lebanese militia group involved in the intricacies of Middle Eastern politics. The governments of several states had declared him an outlaw and he and his followers were now best described as bandits with terrorist tendencies.

Chang looked up. 'Nothing on Simmonds?'

'No. I'm assuming your magnificent databases will turn up something.'

'Sarcasm,' he said, 'a sign of insecurity, our profilers tell us. I'll check on him.'

'What do I tell Sabatini?'

'Tell him nothing.'

'What will you tell Ali?'

Chang shook his head, drained his coffee, got up and walked away.

I guessed that we were allies in deceiving our comrades and I remembered what Megan said I had told her about allies.

27

I didn't have to do anything about Sabatini. Rosemary flew back into Sydney and took all his attention. Perhaps he was tired of the waiting game, and he had my assurance that I'd give him everything I had when it came time for him to write a full story. *If* it became time; the international flavour of the names I'd passed on to Chang had me worried that the whole case might move out of state police hands and be taken on by the feds or the intelligence agencies.

I needn't have worried.

'This Simmonds is a consular official in Hong Kong,' Chang told me at our next meeting. We were in Sydney Park in St Peters, walking the paths. The four towers, the lungs of the old brick factory, were casting long shadows and the wind was chill.

'Consular. That means he deals with immigration matters, visas and such.'

'Right. Authorises visas and these days has a role in monitoring applications from skilled people and those with investment capabilities.'

'Passports?'

'Probably has a drawer full of 'em.'

'Does this mean you're going to hand this over to the feds or the spooks?'

Chang, who had a long stride, stopped abruptly. 'Shit, no! Certainly not at this stage. Doesn't take much to put it together, does it? Chinese and Lebanese criminals getting entry to this country through corrupt DFAT officials. They get set up in already existing businesses which have been compromised in some way by Malouf's dealings, and have had pressure put on them by Freddy Wong and Houli. Those two were looking to be part of the ongoing action.'

I said, 'He's a crafty bastard, this guy, only gives us one of the officials and a couple of names. You have to wonder how widespread it is—how many crooks, how many businesses and how big.'

'And how much money.'

We were walking again. 'Cancerous,' I said.

Chang stepped off the path to pick up a soft drink can. He tossed it at a bin; it bounced on the rim but went in. 'It could be. Business is the lifeblood of ethnic communities in this city. It affects everything—family, religion, schools, politics, sport, the lot. If criminal organisations get control of big Chinese and Lebanese businesses—I mean in terms of money and personnel—it'd be a nightmare.'

'It's big, as he said. But you're not going to pass it on higher?'

Chang didn't reply. We reached the pond, took a turn and headed back towards the towers. There was a dog exercise area away to our left and the sounds of the dogs and the children had a calming, normalising effect on me and apparently on Chang, who stopped and looked.

'My people have been here for a hundred and fifty years,' he said. 'They were on the Victorian goldfields and then had the good sense to come to Sydney. They were market gardeners, laundrymen and shopkeepers. My great-great-grandfather fought in World War I. A couple of my great uncles fought in the next war.' He laughed. 'Mind you, a few members of my family were mistaken for Japs and interned. This place isn't perfect, but I love it and I'm fucked if I'm going to let a bunch of foreign sleazebags come in and bugger it up.'

At home, I punched the buttons to disable the alarm and put my key in the lock. I heard a soft footfall and felt something hard and cold in the nape of my neck.

'Open the door and we'll go in. Drop the keys as soon as we're inside and keep your hands where I can see them.'

What I could feel on my neck wasn't the muzzle of a pistol. Bigger. A silencer. I did as he said, and as soon as the door was closed he slammed me against the wall. He was as quick as a cat and before I could catch my breath he had both wrists handcuffed behind my back.

'Sergeant Ali,' I said. 'Sharpshooter.'

'Don't forget it. Move inside, we've got some talking to do.'

We went into the sitting room and I froze as I heard him open a flick knife. He sliced my jacket down the back and pulled both halves clear of my tied wrists. He shoved me into a chair, put the gun and knife within reach and felt in the jacket. Deftly, he pulled out my phone and the recording device. He fiddled with it and swore.

'Where's the disk?'

I looked at him and said nothing.

'Doesn't matter,' he said. 'You did us a great service getting rid of Freddy and Lester.'

'Us?'

'William and me.'

'William Habib, aka Richard Malouf?'

Ali smiled. 'Light dawns. I'm curious, Hardy, what made Stephen Chang suspicious of me?'

'Is he suspicious?'

He sighed. 'You're going to be a nuisance the way I knew you would be. Stephen's been keeping me busy on a variety of things. Some of them touching on . . . what we're talking about now, but I could tell he was holding a lot back. I know you've spoken to William recently.'

As always, Ali was impeccably dressed and groomed. He was handsome, looked fit and clear-eyed—the image of a rising professional policeman. His body language exuded confidence, but I sensed that he entertained a small doubt.

'I did speak to him,' I said, 'and it worries you that you don't know what was said, doesn't it?'

'I said it doesn't matter.'

'I think it does, Karim. You probably don't know that Freddy Wong was getting ready to dispense with Houli. Habib was setting up to double-cross Houli and Freddy Wong. What's to say he won't double-cross you? Hard to find someone to trust, isn't it?'

'You don't know what you're talking about. Shut up and let me think.'

'I'll tell you who to think about—Stephen Chang.'

'Oh, we've already thought about him. Pity, he's a good policeman, but good policemen get killed in the line of duty all the time.'

'Kill him and you'll never draw another peaceful breath.'

'I won't kill him. It'll depend on how things work out, but I think it's most likely that you'll kill him.'

28

'You must have a weapon here somewhere,' Ali said, 'otherwise it could get messy. Let me see.'

His eye drifted to the cupboard under the stairs. He opened the door and felt among the jackets and coats and bits and pieces hanging there.

'Aha.' He pulled out the .22 I'd got from Corbett and had more or less forgotten about. He held it by the end of the barrel.

'A popgun, but it'll do.'

Everyone has a weakness and Karim Ali's was vanity. He couldn't resist telling me how Habib had engineered financial disaster for a large number of sizeable Chinese and Lebanese businesses in Sydney and had arranged bail-out finance which carried penalties that would bring whole conglomerations of family concerns crashing down. I didn't really understand much of it, but I gathered that

Habib could keep all the balls in the air for about as long as he pleased.

Offshore, he had similar grips on DFAT personnel who were in a position to facilitate visas for criminals who wouldn't have got through the first level of screening. The idea was that they'd bring their experience and capital to Sydney and operate an under-the-radar criminal network.

'Worth millions,' he said, almost savouring the word. 'Millions.'

'Dirty money,' I said. 'I thought you had a promising career.'

'Too slow, much too slow.'

'I can see Freddy and Lester and Houli and Talat as enforcers, but I don't see your role.'

The expression on his face was almost a smirk. 'That's the cutest part, I—'

'But Habib changed tack,' I said, 'pardon the pun. He took to his boat and ducked out of the arrangement. Let me guess—he thought he and you didn't need the Wongs and Houli. You kept him abreast of things when the little chink in the plan appeared. He was sighted.'

Ali nodded. 'That was careless. I told him to change his appearance and use the moorings he'd set up, but he had the hots for Sun Ling. Gretchen. Putting it all at risk for a woman. Promising her the earth, and she's a junkie.'

'It's been done before and it'll happen again. He's flakey now; wants to do a deal with Chang.'

'No, he knows I'll have to step in. The only deal he can do now is with me. When this is all up and running I'll be in charge of the unit and Chinese and Lebanese crime will run . . . smoothly.'

I shook my head. 'Megalomania. I don't think you're on very solid ground.'

'Compared to you, I'm on *terra firma*. You know as well as I do that a big-money, dirty-lawyer network operated here until a certain media magnate left us. The WASPS have had their go: it's the wogs' turn now.'

I watched him as he handled my phone very carefully. It wasn't a particularly interesting phone. He acquainted himself with its functions and I suddenly realised why and had to laugh. His hand shot out for his gun before he realised I hadn't moved.

'You're waiting for his call on my phone,' I said. 'You fed him information when he called you. You don't know where he is, do you?'

'Shut up.'

'To use your boss's expression about how Habib handled me, he'll play you like a fish.'

He took two steps and hit me with a hard chop to the side of my neck. I tried to duck but he was too quick and the blow had a paralysing effect. I could breathe and see but I couldn't move.

The phone buzzed. He had the voice message activated, listened, and let the message run out.

'A woman,' he said, 'sounded young. You old goat.'

Probably Megan, I thought. I was developing a contempt blending with my dislike for him and had to fight the feelings down. Such impulses cloud judgement, and I didn't think Ali held all the cards, not yet. The feeling of paralysis receded, but I kept myself in the rigid position I'd been in as it hit me.

The phone rang again; he listened and then he surprised me. He cleared his throat and answered in a very good imitation of my voice.

'Hardy.'

A pause, then he said, 'It's Karim Ali, William. You're not going to do any deals with Chang, you're going to do a deal with me.'

It wasn't hard to guess at Habib's surprise but I had no way to tell what he said except to infer it from Ali's responses. He told Habib to cool down and think and it was a sure bet Habib was doing plenty of thinking. Ali explained that he'd been forced to act because Chang had become suspicious of him.

'He has to be removed.'

Habib must not have liked that because Ali had to go into some detail about how it could all still work with him running things—would work better, in fact.

He told Habib he could arrange to make it appear that I had killed Chang. Habib apparently liked that even less.

'Very well,' Ali said, 'we'll have to discuss all this face to face. I agree there's a lot to consider.'

At a guess Habib said something about his intention to ditch the whole thing in return for immunity because Ali became conciliatory.

'Look, you were under a lot of pressure. It got bigger than we thought too quickly and you were all caught up with that woman. That's water under the bridge. The Wongs are out and that's a plus. We can get some other Chinese in who're more compliant and I can handle Houli. It'll be all right. You can . . . recover her.'

All of a sudden Ali noticed how closely I was following the conversation. He swore, switched to rapid Lebanese, and that was the end of my understanding. The only word I caught in what followed sounded like 'fairchild'.

He hung up and looked me over. Moving quickly he upended the chair I was on, leaving me with my feet in the air. He stripped off his tie and trussed my feet together. Then he righted the chair and went into the kitchen. He returned with a tea towel, cut a long, wide strip from it with his knife and gagged me.

'That'll keep you quiet for a while.' He took a small bottle from his pocket, shook out a pill and swallowed it down dry. He worked his shoulders to loosen them and stretched like a cat. He cleared his throat again and punched a number into the phone. He smiled as the call was answered.

'Inspector, this is Hardy. I'm at my place and I need to talk to you. Can you come over here?'

I'm a fair mimic on a good day, but he was better; and again, I was in the frustrating position of listening to only one end of a conversation. Tied up as I was, it was more stressful this time.

'I don't want to talk about it on the phone. I still think Habib could be picking up signals . . . I don't think it's paranoia . . . I'm worried about Houli . . . Talat? No, I don't know anything more about him . . . OK, as quick as you can, and . . . be careful.'

He cut the call and took a deep breath. The impersonation had been very good, not perfect, but good enough allowing for telephonic distortion. Ali looked pleased with himself as he put the phone down. He went back to the kitchen and got a bottle of wine and a glass.

'We're not supposed to drink alcohol, but then, there's lots of things we're not supposed to do.'

He poured himself a glass of my cut price merlot and sipped it. 'I don't drink enough to tell whether it's good or bad. I suspect it's cheap, like you, like everything people like you do.'

He was nervous, talking *at* me, but *to* himself. Nervous, he was even more dangerous than relaxed. I wondered what the pill he'd taken was, and what effect the wine might have with it. He left the room and I heard the toilet flush. The phone rang, he raced back, swearing, and answered using my voice, perhaps less convincingly.

'What? . . . When? . . . Where did she go? . . . I can't right now . . . Yes, yes, soon as I can.'

Gagging is an art that not many people study. Ali hadn't. I worked my jaw against the strip of cloth and loosened it so that I could push against it with my mouth and tongue. It flopped down.

'It's unravelling, Karim,' I said. 'It's not going to work.'

'Fuck you!' He spilled wine from the glass he'd picked up and threw the rest into my face. His arm jerked back, hit the wall and the glass broke. Blood spurted from his hand.

I licked at the drops around my mouth. 'Thanks,' I said. 'Cut your losses, mate. Get together what you've managed to rip off so far and head for the hills. You'll have left DNA all over the place and you'll never convince the SOC people of the scenario you've got planned.'

'Shut up!'

Red wine stained his white shirt and without his tie he suddenly looked nothing like the in-control executioner he'd seen himself as. He paced up and down, getting more and more agitated. He sucked at the cut on his hand. I hoped someone else would ring to up the stress level but no one did and I had to try to do it myself.

'Turn on the news,' I said, 'maybe they've found Habib on his boat.'

'How did you learn about the boat?'

'Oh, that's right. I left certain things out in that off-the-record chat we had after you shot Lester. Let me think . . . Sun Ling, Gretchen, told me.'

'That crazy junkie bitch.'

'Didn't look crazy to me.'

'She is. She's been in and out of institutions since puberty. Nearly killed a man once. I know what I'd do to her if I . . .'

'What?'

'Never mind. Where *is* that bloody Chang?'

'That was May Ling calling, wasn't it? So Gretchen's on the loose? You should warn Habib, but you can't unless you impersonate me again and, frankly, your last effort wasn't that good.'

He was so close to the edge that he didn't even bother to reply. He took out his phone and looked at it.

'You've got no one to call,' I said, 'no one you can trust. I'm almost sorry for you.'

The doorbell rang. I opened my mouth to shout but, again, Ali was too quick for me. He pulled the gag back into place and hit me with another of his paralysing blows. He picked up the .22 and headed down the passage.

Tasting and breathing dirty tea towel, I closed my eyes. I heard a scuffle and a series of thuds after the door opened but no gunshot. When I opened my eyes Stephen Chang was handcuffing Ali to the stair banister. Ali was fighting for breath; Chang wasn't even puffing. He went down the passage and returned with the small pistol.

'You could get in big trouble for this, Hardy.'

I'd recovered movement enough to nod. Chang untied the gag. He spotted Ali's knife and used it to cut the tie around my feet. Ali stood helplessly and Chang felt in his jacket pocket for the handcuff key. He unlocked the cuffs.

'Stand up slowly,' he said, 'let the blood return to where it belongs.'

I did what he said. 'Traditional Chinese advice.'

'That's right, and this prick copped a traditional Chinese heart punch.'

'How did you know?' I said.

Chang sat and crossed his legs. 'Well, we had our suspicions, didn't we? And when I fished around a bit I found out things I should've noticed before. Just small stuff in his reports; some unexplained gaps in his diary. But what saved your arse was May Ling. I was set to come over here although your voice sounded a bit off. But given your health problems . . . Anyway, May Ling called me and said she was sure someone was impersonating you. She's got a trained ear. A singer, apparently. So I was ready.'

I told Chang about the conversation Ali had had with Habib and the signs of tension between them.

'Any indication of where he is?' Chang asked.

'Not really. When Ali noticed my ears were flapping, he switched to Lebanese.'

'Not really isn't no.'

'I caught a word. It sounded like "fairchild". Mean anything to you?'

Chang shook his head. 'Not a thing. Are we talking about a person or a place?'

Ali's laugh was a hysterical screech. 'You won't find him. He's much too clever for you and the whole fucking—'

He was cut off by my phone ringing again. I answered it.

'Cliff Hardy.'

'Cliff, really you?' May Ling said.

'Really me. I have to thank you—'

'No time. I've just heard from Gretchen. She says she's going to kill Malouf.'

'How? Where?'

'She says he's at a wharf in Fairmild Cove.'

'Where the fuck's that?'

'Mortlake somewhere. I'm going there now.'

'May Ling, don't. Wait. I've got Inspector Chang here. We'll get police there—'

'No, no, you don't understand what she's like. I have to get there first. I'm going. I just wanted you to know.'

She cut the call.

29

I told Chang what May Ling had said. As I did, I grabbed my car keys from a hook in the kitchen.

'What d'you think you're doing?'

'I'm going there. That woman saved my life and yours. And if that's where Habib is that's where I have to be.'

Chang pulled out his phone. 'I can get a unit there quicker than you . . .'

'She says her sister's unstable. Ali here told me she almost killed someone once. A howling siren could set her off. Deal with what you've got here, Inspector, and come along when you're ready.'

'Fuck you, Hardy.'

I left with Chang still swearing and Ali laughing.

The Falcon looked as though half of it had been sitting out in a hailstorm. The passenger side and part of the roof were pitted where the pellets had struck and the windows were chipped. It started perfectly though and I got going. I was tired but adrenalin charged. I had a rough idea of how to get to Mortlake, and I decided I'd search for Fairmild Cove once I got there.

I headed west through light traffic towards Strathfield and picked up the road that went close to the Concord golf course where I'd once had dealings with a client, and on to the outskirts of Mortlake where my sense of direction cut out. I stopped and consulted the *Gregory's*. Fairmild Cove was adjacent to the Mortlake ferry and the way there was well signposted.

I got moving again and things came back to me. Just before I joined the army I decided to get myself super fit so as to be a star recruit. I'd been told that rowing was the best aerobic exercise of the lot, so I joined a rowing club. There were a lot of chaps from private schools but one or two roughies like me. I was put through my paces in a gym first, and I just qualified to be allowed in a boat. I rowed in fours and eights on the Parramatta River for a couple of months. I'd never done anything as strenuous before and never since, including basic training. A hard row takes everything out of you, breaks you down to your fundamental physical capacities. I remembered the area around Mortlake—a complex of jetties and wharves to do with some industrial concern—coal, or was it gas? It then looked, if not derelict, neglected. I wondered how it looked now.

The suburbs were quiet; the residents of Concord and

Mortlake went to bed early or were glued to their flat-screen TVs. Hilly Street took me to the ferry. A sign said it ceased operation at six fifteen pm. Two cars were parked in front of the locked, three-metre high gate. One was May Ling's silver Peugeot; the other was the red Mercedes I'd seen in the garage at the Nordlung house. The ferry was drawn up to the dock and there was no sign of movement.

I had my answer to the changes since I was last here. Where the industrial operations had sprawled, there were blocks of townhouses. One set flanked the river and on the opposite side of the street, with a less expensive view, another was in a late stage of construction. Fairmild Cove was a small sandy beach beside the ferry wharf. A boardwalk ran away to the left, between the townhouses and the river. The moon was high and bright and I could glimpse a jetty poking out into the river a hundred metres away. A sign at the beginning of the boardwalk announced that it was on private property. The public had access, but the sign listed all the things that were banned along its length—almost everything. You could walk a dog on a leash. Forget the dog and it was Habib's milieu all right—waterfront residence with boat facilities.

The boardwalk was well lit but I grabbed a torch from the glove box before setting off—a big torch with heavy batteries. A useful weapon if needed. There were lights on in some of the townhouses and in the warmer months there would probably have been people out on the balconies sipping drinks and taking in the moonlit view. Not tonight, with a cold wind. The water slapped against the rocks at the base of the boardwalk and spray hit the chain that served as a handrail. It had a cold, clammy feel.

I rounded a bend and saw a series of jetties arranged in a rough H pattern. A few boats were tied up, not many. It looked like a perfect place for a marina but as if the idea hadn't yet occurred to anyone. Or maybe the money wasn't in the right pockets yet. I moved forward straining to see or hear anything that might tell me what was happening. The dull pulsing in my damaged ear that I'd grown used to was sharper, affected by the wind.

You're too old for this. Who'd said that? I couldn't remember.

'Hardy!'

May Ling rose up from a crouch near a point where the jetties branched and there was some kind of sculpture providing cover. She grabbed my arm and pulled me down as she pointed.

'They're on that boat,' she whispered. 'I don't know what to do. Help me, help her.'

30

It was possibly the first time in her life that May Ling hadn't known what to do.

'I saw her,' she said. 'Just a few minutes ago. She looked so wild, so mad. She had a gun.'

'What d'you mean, a pistol, a handgun?'

'No, something bigger, longer . . .'

'Like a rifle or a shotgun?'

'I don't know! I don't know! She's capable of anything. I'm so scared. She hates me, she hates herself, she . . .'

'Stay here.' I gave her my mobile. 'Stephen Chang's number's listed. Call him. Tell him what's going on.'

'I've got his number. I don't need your phone. What are *you* going to do?'

I didn't answer because I didn't know. I moved forward, keeping low and out of the pools of light until I reached the short dock where the boat was the only one moored. Under the moonlight I could read the name—*High Five*. It was big, not as big as some, but big enough, with a long mast waving in the wind and several satellite dishes mounted around the superstructure. Lights showed in the body of the boat. I crept closer until I could sort out where the lower deck began and how to reach it. There was an opening near the front where the rail had been folded back and pinioned. The boat was rocking gently; it was securely fastened, but a tide was building, running towards the harbour.

I stepped onto the boat and worked my way back to the deck where there was light. I could hear the faint hum of a generator. I moved clear of the raised section and peered around the corner to the awning-covered space. I couldn't see anything but I heard the unmistakable sound of people fucking—the creaking, the panting. A short set of steps led down to what had to be cabins and a living area.

The action heated up and then stopped abruptly. Sun Ling's voice, breathless, alarmed, disappointed, was an almost hysterical screech.

'Richard, no! Don't stop! Fuck you. I—'

I heard a heavy slap. 'Shut up, you stupid bitch.'

I was crouched at the top of the steps with the pistol in my hand staring down into the dimly lit space. Suddenly it was flooded with light. A man stepped out holding what looked like a machine pistol. He was naked and still half erect.

He looked like the Richard Malouf I'd met but not quite

246

like him. His hair was lighter and the shape of his nose was slightly different.

'William Habib,' I said.

'Hardy, put down the gun.'

'You won't shoot me. You don't have to. Ali's under arrest. You've still got a shot at a deal with Inspector Chang.'

'The gun.'

There are killers like Lester Wong and Yusef Talat but Habib wasn't one of them. He wasn't cruel enough or frightened enough. I tossed the pistol over my shoulder and heard it hit the deck.

'We should talk,' I said.

Habib was only in his middle thirties and he'd been an athlete in more ways than one. I'd thought him vain on our meetings and he'd looked as though he'd taken care of his face and figure. Now, naked, with his penis slackening and holding half-heartedly onto a weapon he didn't want to use, he looked older and diminished.

'You trust Chang?' he said.

'As much as I trust anyone. He just now stopped Ali from killing me.'

'God, I never thought it'd come to this. You can set something up with Chang?'

'I can't guarantee everything you might want, but I'll tell you this—you'll have a better chance with him than on the run with Houli and Talat after you. Is Sun Ling all right?'

The grimace was almost a smile. 'When I called her that she almost bit my head off.'

'She's a troubled woman. Her sister—'

'OK, OK. Gretchen's probably pissed off with me. I seem to have that knack with women.'

He hesitated for a second and then put the machine pistol down. 'I'll put some clothes on and we'll talk.'

He stepped back into the cabin. It seemed too easy and I stayed alert, wishing I had the pistol within reach. I had the torch now feeling like not much of a weapon.

When Habib re-emerged he was a different man. He wore a dark silk shirt, white trousers and white deck shoes. His hair had been swept back and tidied. He bent, picked up the machine pistol, and made a beckoning gesture at the cabin. Sun Ling came out wearing a blue silk dress and what Germaine Greer called 'fuck me' shoes. She tottered, holding a hand up to her face. Habib steered her towards the steps.

'She's insurance,' Habib said. 'She seems to matter to you, Hardy. I'll kill her if I have to, to save myself. You have to understand that. The only person in this whole fucking world I care about is me. Got it?'

He seemed to handle the gun with a new assurance. He looked strong and Sun Ling looked frail.

'I believe you,' I said.

'Right. Let's get up where we can parley. Little Gretchen here shot up while we were talking before and she's in dreamland now, near enough.'

The contempt in his voice underlined what he'd said about his lack of concern for everyone but himself. Trouble was, that included me.

Still carrying his weapon, Habib hauled Sun Ling up the steps and dumped her on a recliner. He looked tired as he sat in one of the aluminium-frame chairs and gestured for me to do the same. I shook my head and leaned back against the rail. I let my eyes drift around, looking for the pistol, but I couldn't see it.

'Not going to do anything silly, are you?' Habib said.

'No. Are you?'

'You know this is an ocean-going vessel and I've taken on enough fuel to get me well out into international waters.'

'Just you and Sun Ling? Is that enough . . . crew?'

He looked down at the woman lying on the recliner. Her eyes were closed; her mouth hung slightly open and a thread of spittle slid down to her perfectly moulded chin. He looked away with an expression of disgust.

'No, just me. Gretchen came intending to kill me with a spear-gun. I persuaded her not to the old-fashioned way. But I don't need the encumbrance. This vessel's state of the art—storm-proof, sink-proof.'

'That's what they said about the *Titanic*.'

He laughed. 'No icebergs in the wide blue Pacific.'

I edged towards him but he touched the gun and I stopped. 'Plenty of sharks, though, and you know the sharks that're really waiting aren't in the water.'

He frowned. 'That's your hole-card, isn't it?'

'I don't play cards. All that stuff bores me, but you and I know there are people in the Middle East and Hong Kong and the tax havens that're very interested in you. Not to mention our locals. They follow the money and if they lose track of the money . . .'

'OK, OK. You think I stand a chance with Chang— immunity, witness protection and all that?'

I studied him. Tired, stressed, he should have been more agitated than he appeared.

'I'm guessing you've got a plan B,' I said. 'You've put money and documents away in various places and reckon you can play another game from behind the official smokescreen.'

He nodded. 'You're speculating. The thing to do now is to drive the best bargain I can. You stay here. There are sensors and cameras all over this boat. That's how I knew you were aboard. Just give me a minute and we'll get this show on the road.'

Sun Ling coughed and appeared to be choking. I bent down to help and heard two thumps which didn't mean anything to me, and another noise that did. A heavy engine thundered into life and the *High Five* churned up the water as it swung away from the jetty and headed out into the river.

31

I ignored Habib's instruction and moved forward to the wheelhouse enclosed in a transparent cocoon. There were dials, screens and switches and flashing lights. Habib stood, with the machine pistol hanging by a shoulder strap, steering the yacht. The engine was purring quietly now, no need to shout. What he'd said about sensors and cameras must have been true because he saw me coming and swung towards me with the gun lifted.

'What the fuck are you doing?' I said.

'I feel safer out here. Call up Chang. We'll put him on the speaker and hear what he has to say. We'll deal or no deal.'

'And what if it's no deal?'

'Then you and Gretchen can swim for the shore and I'm gone.'

'She's in no condition to swim.'

'Too bad. You must have your bronze medallion or whatever they called it back in your day. You can save her. She'd be grateful, Hardy. Believe me, she can show her gratitude. Call Chang!'

The gun was pointed at me and Habib looked poised and confident, in charge of the yacht, the situation. I reached into my pocket for the mobile but it chirped just as I took it out. I answered.

'Hardy, this is Chang. May Ling called me. I'm on a police boat and we've got you in sight. What's going on?'

'Hang on,' I said.

I stepped out of the wheelhouse and looked around the wide, fast-running river. We were in midstream and the lights on either shore looked distant in a rising mist—further than I'd want to swim with someone in tow these days. A blue light cut through the haze and, squinting against it, I saw a water police boat moving quickly towards us.

'Better stay back, Inspector,' I said, loudly enough for Habib to hear. 'Habib's armed and dangerous, but he wants to . . . negotiate.'

Habib did something to the controls and the boat slowed. He came out to the rail and rammed the gun into my kidneys. 'Tell him I have hostages.'

'He has hostages,' I said, 'me and Gretchen Nordlung.'

Chang said, 'We can't communicate like this. I'm coming aboard.'

I told Habib what Chang had said. He shook his head.

'He can come close but not on board. I can get clear of that tub in a few seconds.'

I communicated this to Chang and the police boat drew nearer. Habib reached into the wheelhouse, flicked a switch, and the engine noise became a whisper. The yacht wallowed a little and I gripped the rail.

Habib laughed. 'What's the matter, Hardy? Getting seasick? This is a mill pond.'

'There'll be weapons on that police boat,' I said. 'If I were you I'd put that gun of yours down or you might give the wrong impression.'

'You've got a point. Now you just back off a few steps. That's right.'

As I moved away he unslung the gun and hung it on a hook within easy reach.

'I'm not sure this is going to work,' Habib said. 'Too many eyes and ears. I think . . .'

A sound inside the wheelhouse distracted him. He turned to look and I took two long strides and grabbed the gun. He grappled for it but lost balance as I swung away. I dropped the gun into the river. Sun Ling stepped from the wheelhouse holding my .22. She seemed steady, eye and hand, and trained the pistol on Habib.

'Stand up, Richard,' she said.

Habib struggled to his feet. He leaned back against the rail.

'Don't move a muscle,' Sun Ling said. 'I learned to shoot in the States. I was good at it.'

'Easy, Sunny,' I said.

'You too. Back off.'

'I thought you took a hit, darling,' Habib said.

'I didn't.'

'I've got some if you want it.'

Sun Ling laughed, but the pistol didn't waver. 'We used to make love in his flat up there. He said he'd take me to Venice, Hardy. Venice! But he wasn't going to take me to Venice, was he?'

'No,' I said.

'I heard him. He was going to dump me in the fucking Parramatta River.'

She fired the full magazine into Habib's chest. He sagged against the rail. The police boat crashed heavily into the yacht and Habib went over the rail and into the water.

32

The rest of the important events of that night are sharp in my memory. Sun Ling dropped the pistol and tried to jump into the river but I held her until Chang and some of the water police came on board. She collapsed, and one of the cops who had the right training dealt with her—blood test (I told him she was a diabetic), fluids, blankets.

With his eyes on me, Chang picked up the pistol by the barrel from the deck and dropped it into an evidence bag. Then he went below and I heard him talking urgently on his mobile. I pulled my phone out, intending to call May Ling, but one of the cops shook his head and held out his hand for the phone. I handed it over, dodged around him and went down the steps. Chang was still talking. He stopped and stared at me.

'I'm looking for something to drink,' I said.

Chang told whoever he was talking to to hang on and went through the galley kitchen. He poured a glass of water and handed it to me.

'Touch anything in here, Hardy, and you're in more trouble than you are already—and that's a lot.'

Then it was lights and boats and an ambulance and cop cars with no sirens and an interview room and a statement and exhaustion. I don't remember who drove me home or how my pockmarked car appeared outside the house a day later. Then it was as if a big, impenetrable blanket had been thrown over the whole thing. No one wanted to unscramble the eggs.

The water police searched for Habib's body for several days, or said they did. Sharks are not unknown in that stretch of the Parramatta River.

May Ling and Standish organised a team of doctors, psychologists and psychiatrists and Gretchen was institutionalised without any charges laid or pending. May Ling told me there was a note on a file somewhere that Gretchen would be liable to undergo an official psychological assessment somewhere down the track, but she had plans to get her out of the country before that happened.

Karim Ali was allowed to resign. His record was doctored and silence was bought with a moderate payout and a reference that would permit him to get another job. He'd get a contract in the security network somewhere.

The police had me in their crosshairs. Possession of an unlicensed pistol was a serious offence, especially for someone with my record. Chang never actually made the threat, but his one hint was broad enough. I had to play along with all the arrangements.

Chang told me that a technical team went over the boat as if they were excavating an archaeological site.

'There were layers of stuff,' he said. 'I don't pretend to understand what that means but I gather they had a lot of fun with de-encrypting, breaking firewalls, sifting passwords.'

I shook my head. 'Please don't use words like encrypting.'

Chang smiled. 'Anyway, they found mountains of emails and bank records detailing the businesses Habib had snared and the traps he'd set. I'm talking about here and offshore— the Middle East, the Gulf, Hong Kong, Taiwan, the UK, the EU.'

'What about the DFAT people?'

'Retirements and redundancies in the pipeline.'

'A cover-up.'

'Has to be, but that's not the whole of it. Habib and company had been importing drugs and weapons. The IT people say the documents—manifests, receipts, whatever— are brilliant. The stuff was in a network of self-storage places around the city and suburbs; all apparently legitimate and accessible, if you had the right information. They were starting to branch out into identity theft apparently, plus buying up domain names.'

'Cancerous,' I said.

He nodded. 'It looks as if it got too big for Habib and he came under some pressure when he tried to go solo. That may be why he wanted out. Maybe he did, maybe he didn't. It's hard to tell. Apparently he kept a journal in a code they haven't deciphered yet.'

'So Habib had a lot to bargain with.'

'He did, but his dick did him in.'

'Houli and Talat?'

'Compromised.'

'What does *that* mean?'

'There's full documentation on Houli for tax evasion, fraud and extortion. Habib probably kept that on hold as insurance. He had similar records on Freddy Wong. No wonder they were after him. Talat is subject to deportation as an illegal immigrant with a criminal record. At least two countries would like to extradite him.'

'And a murderer.'

Chang shrugged. I looked at him. 'But?'

'Immunity in return for silence, but walking on eggshells and . . . let's say, potentially useful.'

* * *

I was worried about Sabatini. After the events at Mortlake, all carefully airbrushed by the police with media compliance, I had to tell him something, but he wanted a lot more to allow him to write his story. I stalled. Luckily, he was still so involved with Rosemary that he didn't press too hard, but eventually I had to confront the problem. I consulted Chang.

'I promised,' I said.

'You had no right to.'

'He was helpful.'

'I'll see what I can do.'

In the end it was all of a piece with the rest of it. The investigators agreed to release a certain amount of information. This was traded to Sabatini for an undertaking that his story could be vetted and sanitised. That's how it worked out. I heard later that Sabatini and Rosemary were married. I wasn't invited to the wedding.

None of the money Habib had spirited away came back to me and I was very low on funds. I hadn't spent much of Standish's original advance on the investigation, but I whittled it down quickly afterwards. Then Standish got me off the hook about the shares. It took time— months. I didn't understand how and didn't try to understand. The GFC seemed to be passing us by and Standish insisted on paying me a bonus. It cleared my debts and at least put me on an even footing with all the constant demands of modern city living—the rates, the phone, the power, the RTA and all the rest. I was solvent, but without prospects.

Except for one. Megan was due to give birth and that kind of blotted out all the other problems.